MW00414980

COURTING THE CAT WHISPERER

A Nocturne Falls Universe Story

Copyright © 2018 by Wynter Daniels

This book is a work of fiction and was made possible by a special agreement with Sugar Skull Books, but hasn't been reviewed or edited by Kristen Painter. All characters, events, scenes, plots and associated elements appearing in the original Nocturne Falls series remain the exclusive copyrighted and/or trademarked property of Kristen Painter, Sugar Skull Books and their affiliates or licensors.

Any similarity to real persons, living or dead, is purely coincidental and not intended by the author or Sugar Skull Books.

Published in the United States of America.

Dear Reader,

Nocturne Falls has become a magical place for so many people, myself included. Over and over I've heard from you that it's a town you'd love to visit and even live in! I can tell you that writing the books is just as much fun for me.

With your enthusiasm for the series in mind – and your many requests for more books – the Nocturne Falls Universe was born. It's a project near and dear to my heart, and one I am very excited about.

I hope these new, guest-authored books will entertain and delight you. And best of all, I hope they allow you to discover some great new authors! (And if you like this book, be sure to check out the rest of the Nocturne Falls Universe offerings.)

For more information about the Nocturne Falls Universe, visit http://kristenpainter.com/sugar-skull-books/

In the meantime, happy reading!

Kristen Painter

Welcome to Nocturne Falls, the town where Halloween is celebrated 365 days a year. The tourists all think it's a show: the vampires, the werewolves, the witches, the occasional gargoyles flying through the sky. But the supernaturals populating the town know better.

Living in Nocturne Falls means being yourself. Fangs, fur, and all.

Telepathic petsitter Jordan Vaughn wishes she could forget her checkered past. Despite her genuine efforts to make amends, she falls short every time. When she meets the guy of her dreams, she's sure that her bad-luck streak is over.

A head injury erased Harry Hill's memory. Now, four years later, he's built a new life in Nocturne Falls, complete with a gorgeous girlfriend.

Everything is falling into place—until someone tries to kill him. But will the past he can't remember jeopardize his future with Jordan?

Cover design by Jax Cassidy

COURTING THE CAT WHISPERER

PROLOGUE

Where am I?

God, his head ached something awful. And his left arm. He inhaled the pungent smell of decaying leaves. Was he dreaming?

His eyes felt gluey as he opened them. But he still couldn't see anything.

An owl hooted nearby, and the sound of birds flapping their wings came and went. No, not birds—bats.

His lower back protested as he eased himself into a sitting position. The sky was murky and black. No moon, lots of clouds.

Why was he there?

Something warm pushed against his side. He jerked away, which incited a fresh round of pain—his wrist, his neck.

A cat? Yes, a white one with a darker mask around its eyes. It purred and nudged his arm.

He let out the breath he'd been holding. As his eyes adjusted to the darkness, he glimpsed the trunk of a fallen tree a few feet away. And a steep wall of rock.

"How did I get here, cat?"

The animal started away then stopped and meowed at him. What was it trying to tell him?

Lightning lit up the sky. Seconds later, a boom of thunder. The air cooled. He pulled his collar tighter around his neck. A storm would only worsen his situation.

But what was his situation?

The cat trilled, imploring him to follow. It wasn't as if he had a better plan, so he used the tree trunk to pull himself up. His head pounded, and both of his wrists were tender. Every muscle in his body complained. Why was he so sore?

He started after the feline, swallowing past the dryness in his throat. "I don't suppose you know what happened to me, hmm? Or how long I've been here."

The cat stopped, waited for him to catch up, then continued through the woods, over rocks and fallen branches. They climbed higher and higher until they reached a flat area.

"I've got to rest," he told his four-legged guide. Why was he so weak? He sat on the ground, and the cat joined him as if it understood.

"What's your name, kitty?" He smoothed the silky fur on its back as it purred in response. "I'll call you..." He had no idea. It dawned on him that he didn't know his own name. In fact, he couldn't remember anything about himself—where he lived, his age, nothing. All he did know was that he had the mother of all bumps on the back of his head and several cuts and scrapes. He ran his fingers over the abrasion on his left arm and felt a newly-formed scab there. And although he couldn't see it well, he was sure there was a bruise on his right wrist. How long had he been unconscious?

Getting to his knees, he patted his pant pockets. No wallet, no keys. No answers.

Another clap of thunder shook the ground. Sheets of rain instantly soaked his clothes.

The cat sat beside him, consoling him.

"Who am I?" he asked it. His stomach growled. When was the last time he'd had anything to eat? Chills racked his body.

He smoothed the cat's wet fur. It pawed at his right front pocket. "What is it?" Sliding his fingers into the pocket, he felt something. He pulled out a damp, folded paper. Carefully opening it, he tried to make out what it said, but in the dark, it was impossible to read.

The cat's ears perked up a second before the man heard the distinctive hum of a vehicle. Headlights hopscotched from tree to tree. "We must be close to a road," he said to the cat. He stood up, but the vehicle was gone. Only the sound of the falling rain remained.

When the cat scampered away, the man offered up a silent prayer that it was going to lead him to civilization. He carefully slipped the paper back into the pocket of his shirt then followed the cat.

They walked for ten or twelve minutes, finally reaching asphalt. "Good kitty," he said as the feline sat down at his feet. Within a few minutes, another vehicle drove toward them. He waved, and after that failed to get the driver to slow down, he started flailing his arms. But the car whooshed past at high speed, splashing water on the man and his cat.

He glanced down at the kitty. "Are you mine?"

It purred and rubbed against his shins.

"There's my answer." Minutes ticked past. Finally, another vehicle approached, slowing down as it came closer.

The driver lowered his passenger window a couple of inches. He was elderly with white hair and red-rimmed blue eyes. "What are you doing out here, son?"

For a moment, he wondered if the old man was someone he knew—his father, or grandfather. "Are you—?"

"You need a lift somewhere?" the octagenarian asked.

Wherever he was, he did need a way out of there. Didn't matter where the old man was heading. "I...yes, please."

"Get in then." The driver pushed open the passenger door.

"Thanks."

The cat jumped inside ahead of him.

4

The senior man chuckled and petted it. "Well hello there." He pointed to the seatbelt. "Buckle up, would you?"

"Sure." He strapped himself in as the older man pulled back onto the pavement. "Do you know where we are?"

"Right smack in the middle of nowhere." Another laugh. "'Bout twenty miles past Murrayville."

Murrayville? He wished that rang a bell. Then he remembered the paper he'd stuck in his pocket. He took it out, but it was so wet that most of the ink had run together. Another vehicle passed them going the opposite direction, its headlights illuminating the letter for a brief moment. He was able to make out a few letters at the top right of the page—"Harr." Harry? Was that him? If so, he had no idea if it was his first or last name. "What state is this?"

The old man narrowed his eyes at him. "Georgia. You all right?"

Not really. "Just a little thirsty."

The old man flattened his lips. "I'm Jim Turner. What's your name?"

He wished he knew. They passed a sign warning of a steep hill ahead. "Harry," he said. "Harry Hill. And the cat's name is…Kitty."

The man snickered. "Very original. How'd you get that cut over your eye, Harry?"

His hand automatically went to the spot. "I'm not sure."

The man mumbled something under his breath. "Maybe I should drop you at a hospital. Next one's about an hour's drive."

He shook his head. "I feel okay."

The older man gripped the steering wheel with both hands. "I'm headed to my daughter's place just past Nocturne Falls. I'll drop you anywhere along the way."

"Nocturne Falls?" he asked.

"The place where it's Halloween every day. Nice little town."

No, he didn't know. He shrugged. "Sure, why not?" He just hoped that in the light of day he'd figure out who the hell he was.

CHAPTER ONE

Four years later...

I will not screw this up.

Jordan Vaughn checked the time on the wall clock in her sister's kitchen before slipping a pan of bacon into the oven. She had to leave for her petsitting gig in less than an hour to feed all the cats by nine. Her client had stressed that the kitties would be very unhappy if they didn't eat first thing in the morning.

Jordan wasn't nearly as proficient at multitasking as her twin, but how many times had she watched Mallory cook breakfast, pack a lunch, and feed the dog and cat — all while putting on her make-up?

Her twin loved to joke that Jordan couldn't even get a glass of water without making a mess, but today she'd prove Mallory wrong. Today marked one year since Mal had met her fiance, so Jordan was determined to surprise them with a home-cooked breakfast. After all, Jordan owed the couple her very life after they'd rescued her from a dastardly duo who'd kidnapped her last year.

She probably should have set her alarm for an hour earlier, though. After switching on the burner under the frying pan, she cracked four eggs into a bowl and started beating them.

Hazel—Mallory's cat—hissed. Then the dog growled. What were those two up to? If they didn't pipe down, they'd wake Mal and Cyrus before Jordan had their breakfast ready. She rolled her eyes as she set aside the eggs then headed into the living room to deal with the animals. "What's goin on, guys?"

He took my catnip mouse, Hazel silently told her.

Did not, Truffle insisted.

Jordan spotted the toy behind the Yorkie. "Truffle, give it back to her, please. I don't have time for an argument this morning."

The pup scurried away, and Hazel immediately pounced on the mouse. Thanks, Jordan.

"Don't mention it." The moment she started from the room, an eardrum-popping screech exploded all around her. The smoke detector? And what was that smell? Something was burning. Oh, God!

Gasping, she raced back to the kitchen. Thick black smoke filled the air. She shut off the stove, grabbed a dishtowel and wet it before opening the oven. Flames poured out, engulfing her.

"What's going on?" Mallory waved away the smoke and slammed the oven door shut. "What have you done now?"

Cyrus shoved Jordan out of the way as he grabbed a fire extinguisher from under the sink and doused the flames.

Mal yanked open the front door. "Turn on the exhaust fan," she called to no one in particular.

Jordan did as her sister asked. Stepping back, she surveyed the disaster she'd caused. The entire place reeked of burnt bacon. A huge black stain covered the top of the stove and the wall behind it.

"My beautiful kitchen." Mallory sank into a kitchen chair and sniffled.

Cyrus wrapped Mallory into his arms. "If I still had my magic, I could clean this up in no time flat." But he'd lost his powers last year after Mal had wished for him to be a genie no longer.

Jordan gulped. "I was going to surprise you both with breakfast in bed. For your anniversary."

Mal smoothed back her long blond locks. "You succeeded in surprising us. That's for sure."

Clenching her jaw to keep herself from crying, Jordan kneeled in front of her sister.

"I'm so sorry. What can I do to make this up to you?"

Mal just shook her head. "Not now, Jordan."

Standing, Jordan nodded. "Would you rather I just left?"

Cyrus patted her shoulder. "That'd probably be a good idea."

Resisting the urge to cry, Jordan picked up her suitcase from the front hall and walked out.

Would she ever be able to do anything right? She'd screwed up time and again in her relationship with Mallory. In truth, she'd envied her twin as far back as she could remember. In school, Mal had always made better grades than Jordan, and even though they were identical, boys had flocked around Mallory, while they'd mostly ignored Jordan.

Until that day during their senior year when Mallory's then-boyfriend had started flirting with Jordan.

Of all her regrets, Jordan's greatest was taking up that cheater on his lewd proposition. No matter how many times she'd apologized to Mallory, her sister had never truly forgiven her for the egregious betrayal. Jordan couldn't blame her.

The very least Jordan could do was to move out of Mal's house as soon as possible, not only to give the couple the privacy they deserved but also to prove to her parents and her sister that she could stand on her own two feet. Her dog-walking and pet-sitting service hadn't taken off as well as she'd hoped, and she was barely making ends meet. All she could do was pray that her luck was changing. After the service that the Tuckers had originally hired for the job canceled at the eleventh hour, Mrs. Tucker had phoned Jordan last night. Jordan had jumped at the opportunity to make a nice chunk of change, plus the job would give her some long-overdue alone time.

Fifteen minutes after she'd left Mal's place, she parked her Smart Car on Eerie Avenue then double checked her phone for the address Mrs. Tucker had texted her. Yup, this was it. She whistled as she took in the bay windows, the twin turrets, and the beautiful wraparound porch. The Victorian-style home was easily five times the size of Mallory's house, which was actually quite spacious. But this...this was stunning. Little had she known when she agreed to take this job that the Tuckers lived in a virtual mansion. Score!

She grabbed her suitcase from the trunk and headed up the walk. Mrs. Tucker had said she would leave a key under the doormat, but when Jordan checked, she found nothing but a few dead leaves. She set her bag on a wicker loveseat and tried calling her. But she went straight to voicemail.

Hmm. A black cat appeared in the bay window. Perhaps he knew where his mistress had put the key. Thank goodness Jordan could telepathically communicate with animals.

She tapped on the glass to say hello. "I'm Jordan," she told him, "I'll be staying with you while your people are away."

Another cat joined him on the sill, an orange tabby, so Jordan introduced herself to him as well. "How many of you live here?" she asked it.

Six, the black one silently told her.

Plus four kittens, the tabby added.

"Wow, no wonder she wants me to stay here while she's away." She scooted closer to the window. "One problem, though. Your mistress promised to leave me a key, but I can't find it. Do either of you know where it is?"

Nope.

Sorry.

How was she going to get <u>inside</u>?

The peoples' bedroom window is open a little. You could climb through it, the tabby told her.

I did that once after I got out of the house, the black cat said. Climb up the ladder next to the porch.

Ladder? She glanced at a rose-covered trellis and gulped. Sure, it would make a perfect ladder for a cat, just not for a person. "There must be another way."

I don't think so, the tabby said.

Come on, the black cat said. We're hungry. The kittens are whining. We need you.

Maybe she could stand on a chair then hoist herself up to the balcony. "Okay, I'll get in," she assured them. Somehow. Maybe there was an actual ladder around back. But after a thorough search of the yard, she didn't find anything to help her reach the second story.

Three black and white kittens appeared in the window next to the back door. She tried the doorknob. Locked.

Two of the kittens pawed the glass. Feed us, they said.

Darn. She had to get inside. The upstairs window looked to be her only option. So she returned to the front of the house and offered up a silent prayer that the trellis was stronger than it appeared. The hardest part would be making it to the edge of the roof over the porch. From there, the balcony was only a few more feet farther, albeit steeply slanted.

Drawing a deep breath, she climbed onto the porch railing then took hold of the trellis. Three rungs up, she managed to grab the rain gutter. She stilled at a popping sound and felt the gutter detach from the eave. "No!" She clawed at the shingles. Part of the trellis snapped. Her left foot caught the rung below.

I'm too young to die.

"I'll catch you."

Chancing a glance below her, she sighed with relief when she found a dark-haired guy running toward the house. Where had he come from? "Oh, thank God."

"Just let go," he urged.

She gulped. What if he missed or dropped her? Not only would she get hurt, but so might he. Her feet were at least three or four feet above his outstretched arms.

"It'll be all right. I promise."

How could she doubt that voice? It was so sure and deep, like an angel of rescue. Heart thundering against her ribs, she offered up a prayer that neither of them would get hurt — or worse. Before she had a chance to think about letting go, the snap of wood galvanized her fear. Part of the trellis snapped, deciding for her.

Time stood still as she dropped like a stone. She was going to die. Oh, how she regretted that she'd never fallen in love, nor gotten the forgiveness she sought from her twin.

The blonde crashed into Harry's arms, knocking them both over the railing and onto the ground. She just lay there, face down on the grass.

His heart lodged in his throat. "Are you all right?"

When she raised her head to look at him, he released the breath he hadn't realized he'd been holding. The woman had the most stunning eyes — sparkling azure blue and ringed with thick, dark lashes. Even with bits of grass in her long hair and dirt smudges on her face, she was beautiful. Her black t-shirt had slipped off her left shoulder, revealing creamy, white skin. But too quickly, she righted her top and sat up. "I think I'm fine." She gave him a smile, which somehow made her even prettier. "You saved my life."

She sure didn't look like a criminal, but why else would she have been trying to climb into a house that didn't belong to her?

If he called the cops on her, they'd probably want to question him, too. He'd steered clear of the law since he'd arrived in Nocturne Falls. He'd always wondered if the bruises he'd had around his wrists for the first few days after he'd awakened had been caused by handcuffs. Not knowing if he had a criminal past, he didn't dare open that can of worms. "What were you doing?" he asked her.

She brushed debris off her jeans and stood up. "Trying to get in. The owners were supposed to leave a key under the mat. They didn't."

Oops. Mr. Tucker hadn't said a word about anyone else needing that key. Last night, on Harry's way home from his previous job, he'd stopped by the DIY Depot and picked up some supplies for the Tucker's renovation project and dropped them at the house. "I'm sorry. That's my fault. I took the key."

"You?" She narrowed her eyes at him then backed away almost imperceptibly. "Why?"

"They hired me to do renovations to the house while they're away."

She huffed. "Well, thanks a lot. I could have been killed trying to get inside."

So much for gratitude.

Poking her index finger at the house, she scowled. "And all those poor cats are famished. I need to get in there, now."

How could he be sure she was who she claimed? What was it about the bossy blonde that seemed familiar? Over the past week, he'd sensed that someone had been watching him. Not that he'd actually seen the person.

It was more of a feeling. Could it have been her? Maybe he'd glimpsed her for a split second, and like a subliminal message, the memory was just out of reach.

He'd done lots of research on the subconscious mind in the last four years, hoping to find a way to remember his old life. But so far he hadn't been able to recall anything. Or maybe he was just paranoid. With good reason, though. A week ago, someone had broken into his mailbox and stolen his mail. Then a couple of days later, he'd found the driver's window of his truck smashed. The vandal had also rummaged through his glovebox. Last night, he thought he'd seen someone peering at him through his bedroom window, although he might have dreamed that. He'd assumed that if someone was trying to mess with him, the culprit was a man. Yet there was no reason it couldn't be a woman.

He rubbed his chin. "So you're supposed to be taking care of the cats?"

"Mm-hmm. Mrs. Tucker phoned me after her regular petsitter crapped out on her." She held out her palm. "May I have the key? I've never been in the house, and I need to find the cat food."

"The owner never said anything about a pet sitter."

She set her hands on her hips and frowned. "Look, Mrs. Tucker is paying me to mind the cats. How do I know that you didn't just steal that key to rob the place?" She folded her arms over her chest and stuck out her chin.

He had to admit—petulant looked adorable on her. But why take a chance when he could easily check out her story. "Excuse me for a moment." Turning his back on her, he phoned the homeowner. After a very brief conversation with a jetlagged Mr. Tucker, he hung up and returned his cell to his pocket.

"Will you let me in now?" the young woman asked.

He faced her and offered his hand. "Please forgive me. You can't be too careful these days. I'm Harry Hill."

After a momentary hesitation, she shook hands with him. "Jordan Vaughn."

He held on a little longer than necessary before letting go then tipped his chin at the front door. "Shall we?"

She gave him a wary nod. "Let me grab my things."

"Allow me." He picked up her battered suitcase and unlocked the door. "Mr. Tucker said there's an extra key on a hook in the kitchen so we can each have one to use."

Inside the foyer, she stopped and glanced around, oohing and aahing at the antique grandfather clock and the massive crystal chandelier. Two black and white kittens rushed in and sniffed at her ankles. She picked one up and cradled it in her arms. "How long will you be working on the renovations?"

He thought about all the items on the Tuckers' list. Refinishing all the built-in bookcases in the study and the living room would take at least a week. The kitchen repairs alone were another week-long project. He also had to refurbish many of the Victorian-style embellishments on the exterior of the house. "About a month. Maybe less."

She sat on a red velvet upholstered bench and ran her hands over the fabric. "Sounds as if it'll be noisy here."

"I'll do my best to keep it down." When he threw her a wink, a pretty pink blush rose in her cheeks.

More cats joined her on the seat and nuzzled her as if she was their long-lost mother. "What's your name, sweet girl?" Then she nodded as if the feline had answered her question. "Nice to meet you, Rosin, Theo. Aren't you a pretty boy, Milo."

How'd she know which was which? He could have sworn she'd said that she'd never been there before. Maybe he'd misunderstood. "Where would you like me to put your suitcase?"

Before answering, she eyed one of the adult cats. Then she looked at Harry. "The guest room. First door at the top of the stairs, on the left."

"Do you know the Tuckers well?" he asked her.

She shook her head. "Yesterday, when Mrs. Tucker called me, was the first time we'd spoken. And the only, so far."

As he carried the suitcase to her room, he wondered if the gorgeous blonde was a little off. She almost seemed to be carrying on a conversation with the cats. Was she delusional? Or just weird? At least she did appear to be a cat person. But clearly, she was also very impressed with the house.

Could Jordan have somehow been behind the Tuckers' regular pet sitter backing out of the job at the last minute?

Not my problem.

Except that he hated unanswered questions. His entire past was a big, fat blank. Living with that gaping hole in his life had made him suspicious of almost everyone. The last thing he needed in his life was a mysterious woman, no matter how attractive.

CHAPTER TWO

After Jordan fed the cats, she went upstairs to unpack. The guest room was huge. She didn't usually care for wallpaper, but the pink and green floral pattern fit with the vintage feel of the house. Milo jumped onto the bed and curled up in Jordan's open suitcase.

"All done eating?" she asked the cat.

Milo started purring. *Thanks for feeding us.*

"My pleasure." She hung her sundress in the closet.

Who's the man downstairs?

"A carpenter. He's doing some work on the house for your people." Jordan arranged her toiletries on the antique vanity.

Milo kneaded her dog and cat pajamas. *Is he your boyfriend?*

"Ha! Definitely not." Harry was a hottie for sure, but she wasn't interested. Not even his incredible sea-green eyes or those amazing shoulders and arms would sway her. Nope. A boyfriend was the last thing she needed. She'd made such terrible choices in her love life as far back as she could remember, which was why she was taking a sabbatical from dating.

"This is a beautiful house," she said. But Milo was asleep. Rather than disturb the cat,

21

she opted to finish unpacking later. Instead, she quietly left the room and went downstairs to explore her temporary home.

To the left of the foyer, she found a large dining room with a mahogany table that would seat at least twelve. Did the Tuckers host dinner parties there? Or family events? From all the family photos that hung on the walls in the hallway and the foyer, Jordan surmised that the Tuckers had several adult children and even a few grandkids. They appeared to have a full life, and judging by their home — and the fact that they were vacationing in Europe for an entire month — a comfortable one.

Jordan sat at the head of the table. Mallory and Cyrus would probably have loads of kids. They both loved children. "And I'll be the spinster aunt," she said aloud.

"Why is that?"

Jordan startled at Harry's question. She pushed away from the table and stood. "I was…" Heat crawled up her neck and face. "Sorry, I didn't know you were around. Sometimes I talk to myself."

"So do I." He shrugged. "People who spend a lot of time by themselves do that."

"I suppose that's true." Why in the world would Harry be alone? With his leading-man good looks, he probably had women falling all over themselves to go out with him. He had the kind of face that would stop a woman in her tracks, but Jordan sensed he wasn't aware of how handsome he was, how mesmerizing his green eyes were. And that body. His shoulders and chest were broad and roped with muscle — the kind that came from hard work, and not from lifting weights at a gym.

"Want to join me for lunch?" He held up a large paper bag she hadn't noticed before. "I ordered burgers and fries from Howler's. Best in town."

Her mouth watered at the thought. "Really? Sure you have enough?"

He waved her into the kitchen. "I figured you might be hungry."

They sat at the small table in the kitchen and Harry unpacked the bag. "Have you had hamburgers from Howler's? They're huge."

"I go there all the time." She bit off half a French fry.

Poking his finger at her, he nodded. "That must be why you look so familiar. I do, too."

"Sounds as if you're as bad a chef as I am." She used a plastic knife to cut her burger in half.

He swallowed his food before responding. "I love to cook. Seems like a waste to do it for one, though."

The knowledge that he didn't have a woman in his life to cook for shouldn't matter to her.

"I eat out a lot—Salvatore's Pizza, Big Daddy Bones, Franks-n-Steins, and of course, Howler's. Or I order out."

"I wish I'd ordered out this morning," she said.

"Huh?"

She rolled her eyes then told him about setting Mallory's kitchen on fire.

"I'll be remodeling the Tuckers' kitchen. Do me a favor and don't use it after I've finished."

"Everything in here?" She glanced around the room. "I only need the fridge and microwave. Clearly, all stoves hate me."

"The appliances are staying. Talk nice to them, and they won't bite."

"As long as they don't spontaneously combust."

He laughed. "You're funny."

"So are you."

"You've got some ketchup..." He pointed to her mouth then shook his head and picked up a napkin. "May I?"

She nodded and held her breath.

Harry dabbed the napkin to her upper lip, lingering there for several moments. He looked into her eyes.

The temperature in the room rose a dozen degrees.

Finally, he backed away.

"What do I owe you for lunch?"

"Nothing. I think there's this rule about when you save someone's life."

"Oh?"

He ate his last French fry. "Seriously. If you save someone's life, then you're responsible for them after that."

"Like forever?" She couldn't hold back a smile.

"I think so. But you're my first rescue, so I'll have to brush up on the rules."

Aside from being funny, and really nice to look at, he seemed interested in everything she had to say. A lot of guys spoke to her as if she were a dumb blonde, a term she hated. She'd met her share of brunettes and redheads who were seriously deficient in the brains department.

Truth was, she'd never thought of herself as particularly smart. Mallory had been an A student all through school, while Jordan had been lucky to make Cs. But it was nice to have a good-looking man pay her some attention. "I like hanging out with you."

Harry's eyes sparkled. "Same here."

A pleasant ache settled in her belly. For heaven's sake. She'd known Harry mere hours, and she was already crushing on the guy. Why bother, though? She'd screwed up every relationship she'd had with men.

Pushing away from the table, she started gathering their trash.

"Let me," Harry said.

"Nope." She waved him away. "You bought, I clean up. That's my rule."

"No argument here." He checked his phone. "I should get back to work."

For the rest of the afternoon, Harry made lots of noise, tearing out cabinets and shelving. Jordan played with the cats, explored the house, and caught up on her social media sites.

A few minutes after five, Harry came into the study carrying his red toolbox. "Guess I'll see you tomorrow."

"Yup, I'll be here." In truth, the prospect of being around him for the next month sweetened the catsitting job.

He combed his fingers through his hair. "Do you have any big plans for the evening?"

Did he plan to ask her out? A fluttering sensation started in her stomach. "Nope, just catching up on a few TV shows, eating one of the yummy frozen dinners she'd brought with her."

He gave her that ridiculously sexy smile. "What a party animal."

Her cheeks warmed. "Yeah, that's me. What about you? Got a hot date?"

"Um, yeah."

Her heart fell.

"A hot date with my cat."

She drew a relieved breath. Not that Harry's love life was any of her concern. "Well, I hope the two of you have a lovely evening."

After a few moments, he took a step toward the foyer. "Thanks. No more climbing on the trellis, okay?"

She saluted him. "I promise."

Once Harry had left, the evening dragged on, and despite Jordan's efforts to keep her mind off of the sexy contractor, he was all she thought about. When sleep refused to come, she blamed it on her unfamiliar surroundings, even though she could usually nod off just about anywhere. Her restlessness didn't have a thing to do with Harry. Absolutely nothing. At some point, she did catch a few zees. Too bad the kittens had awakened her at the ungodly hour of 6:15 am.

By the time she showered and got dressed, it was only a little past seven. She fed the cats then kept glancing out the front window, hoping each car she heard outside was Harry's. Okay, maybe she was a little excited to see him. Only because he was someone to talk to, some company. He was safe—a short-term friend. After her petsitting gig wound up, and his renovation work ended, they'd go their separate ways. End of story.

She returned to the kitchen to start a pot of coffee. The high tech, European machine was fancier than any Jordan had ever used. When she finally figured out how to work it, the thing sputtered and hissed loud enough to wake the dead. And this being Nocturne Falls, it was possible that some of the neighbors weren't a hundred percent alive.

"Good morning."

Jordan jumped at Harry's greeting. Setting a hand over her heart, she smiled at him. "I didn't hear you come in."

"I'm sure. That coffee maker is ridiculously noisy," he said.

"Tell me about it."

He held up a white bakery box with *Delaney's Delectables* stamped on top.

Her mouth watered at the heavenly aroma of fresh-baked pastries. Harry brushed past her, and she detected his piney cologne, which whet an entirely different appetite than the sweets. Clearing her throat, she gestured at the coffee machine. "Can I interest you in a latte?"

A sexy grin lifted one corner of his mouth. "I brought my own, thanks. I hope you like cinnamon-hazelnut danish or maple crullers. It wasn't easy limiting myself to only two." He slapped his flat abdomen. "Too much sugar in the morning slows me down."

"Either sounds delicious. You didn't have to bring me anything."

He opened the box and sniffed. "Mm. It would have been downright cruel of me to eat one of these in front of you without sharing." Grabbing two napkins, he placed each confection on one then cut both pastries in half. "Let's share."

"Thank you." She joined him at the table and spooned sugar into her gourmet coffee.

Harry tipped his chin at her mug. "If that's not the best cup of coffee you've ever had, then the Tuckers got ripped off. Those machines cost more than I make in a week."

She took a sip. "It's good, but honestly, The Hallowed Bean's is better."

Harry chuckled. "As I suspected. Although it'd be tough to beat The Hallowed Bean's Dracu-Latte."

"True." He ate his half of the cruller in two bites, moaning and rolling his eyes heavenward as he did. "Oh, my God! That's amazing."

Ignoring her lack of appetite, Jordan tried the pastry. It was even better than the ones a pastry chef she briefly dated used to make. "Wow, yeah. Spectacular."

"Spectacular," He repeated, but she suspected he wasn't referring to the cruller. His wink incited a butterfly riot in the pit of her belly.

Somehow, she managed to breathe. "What are you working on today?"

"More tear outs. Do you need me to do something?" He licked powdered sugar off his lips.

Heat bloomed inside her. She went to the fridge and got a few ice cubes for her coffee. "No, I was just wondering. I've got a couple of errands to run, so I'll be out for a bit. If you need any help later, let me know."

"I appreciate the offer." Harry wiped down the table. "Speaking of work, I should get on it."

Jordan returned her uneaten half danish to the box as Harry washed his hands. She skimmed her gaze from his broad shoulders to his narrow waist, down those long legs. She couldn't allow herself to get too carried away. Sure, his assets were amazing, but she hardly knew him. Every guy she'd dated since high school had been completely wrong for her. Why should she think that her guy meter had changed? Plus, she had a bad habit of screwing up relationships.

Besides, getting involved with any guy right now was a bad idea. She needed to concentrate on building up her business, not spend her time and energy on some meaningless fling. How would her sister and her parents ever respect her if she couldn't stand on her own feet financially?

While Harry went to fetch his tools, Jordan went upstairs to get ready to leave. Grabbing her purse, she waved to Milo and Theo, who were both curled up on her bed. "I'm going out for a couple of hours, guys."

The felines didn't stir.

Downstairs, she glanced through the doorway into the living room, but Harry was nowhere to be found. She drove to another client's home to walk a chihuahua then picked up an ornery Great Dane and took him to the dog park for exercise. Next, she headed downtown in search of a small gift for Mallory, something that would say, "I'm sorry for destroying your kitchen."

Cruising past Delaney's Delectibles, she shook her head. Mal was dieting ahead of shopping for her wedding gown. When Jordan noticed a florist, she immediately parked and went inside.

The place was so colorful and happy, with all sorts of beautiful bouquets and plants. A pretty blonde came out from the back and gave Jordan a warm smile. "Welcome to Enchanted Garden. Can I help you?"

"I hope so," Jordan said. "I need to send my twin an apology flower arrangement."

The woman laughed. "I'd be happy to whip that right up for you."

Ten minutes later, Jordan left the shop with the prettiest bouquet she'd ever seen. In her car, she jotted a simple, "I love you," then drove over to Mal's house and left the arrangement on the porch.

When she returned to the Tuckers' place, she noticed Harry's white pickup truck out front with *Hill's Carpentry and Renovations* printed on the side.

Knowing he was still there shouldn't have excited her in any way. Her heart did that little fluttery thing at the very thought of being around him. Inside the house, the kittens and cats greeted her with meows and shin rubs. She crouched to give each one a pet or a head scratch.

"Well, hey," Harry said with that southern drawl as smooth and dark as blackstrap molasses. In his green work shirt and jeans faded in all the right places, he looked yummier than anything she'd seen in the window of Delaney's Delectables a little while earlier.

"Hi. How's the construction going?"

"I'm just tearing out some rotted wood this morning." He combed his fingers through his glossy brown hair. "After that, I'll start work on the kitchen, unless you'd rather I do the living room first. If you were going to cook or something."

She stood up and chuckled. "I don't cook. Ever. Thank goodness most of the restaurants in town deliver."

He folded his muscular arms over his chest and gave her a ridiculously sexy grin. "Well then, I'll have to cook lunch for you tomorrow. I make a mean Monte Christo."

Impressive. "Did your mother teach you to cook? Or were you a chef in a former life?"

A cloud passed over his face. "I have no idea." He left the room without any further explanation.

Had she said something wrong? Perhaps he was merely anxious to get back to work. Shrugging, she went upstairs to get her laptop so she could check her social media sites for leads. But a few minutes into her Facebook experience, a rhythmic pounding started shaking the walls. Thump after thump had Jordan's teeth chattering. When it kept on, she teased aside the curtain and smiled at the sight of the expansive yard, complete with a kidney-shaped pool. All the tension escaped her shoulders as she changed into her bikini. Tying a towel around her waist, she grabbed her tube of sunscreen then headed downstairs.

"Sorry if the noise disturbed you." Harry set down a crowbar on the kitchen counter. Pieces of wood molding littered the floor near the stove. "The seventies were alive and well in here. But I've removed most of the vestiges." His gaze trailed down her body then back up to her eyes. An appreciative grin settled on his lips.

The heat of awareness stormed through her. She tightened the towel around her waist.

"Taking advantage of the pool, hmm? Perfect day for it. It's got to be eighty degrees out there."

"Um, yeah." Even with the air conditioner running in the house, she was hot, thanks to Harry's sea-green eyes, and the way he was looking at her as if she were some decadent confection like the ones they'd eaten for breakfast. She swallowed then hurried out the back door.

The pool beckoned to her. Dropping her towel on a lounge chair, she took in the lush trees that surrounded the yard, and the potted flowers on the deck—impatiens, lavender, and marigolds. Nice and private. She slathered lotion on her skin then jumped into the pool. The cool water felt like heaven as she swam to the other side and back again. After a few more laps, she climbed out and made herself comfortable on the lounger.

Closing her eyes, she inhaled the soothing scent of lavender. And pictured Harry peeling off his t-shirt.

His chest and shoulders were even better than she'd imagined—hard and roped with muscle. He stripped down to a pair of black briefs before diving into the water. Then he hauled himself out and stood over her, staring down at her. His wet skin glistened in the sun, making him appear all the more like a buff Greek god.

A rustling sound tore her out of her daydream. She opened her eyes and sat up, scanning the perimeter of the yard. The branches of a nearby Hawthorne bush shifted despite the lack of a breeze. A chill skittered up her spine. Could someone be spying on her?

She glanced toward the house, which was strangely quiet, considering how noisy Harry had been only a few moments earlier.

Bolting off the chair, she wrapped the towel around her body and crossed the lawn to the wooded edge near a small garden shed. "Hello?" she said. "Anybody there?"

Nothing.

"Harry?"

Leaves crunched as if someone was walking past. Jordan held her breath until the sound receded.

A frightening memory flashed in her brain. *She'd been alone at Mallory's old cottage, brushing her hair in front of the mirror when that awful man had broken into Mal's bedroom window. Jordan hadn't had time to think or react as he grabbed her and covered her head with a burlap sack. He'd tied her up, tossed her into the trunk of a car and driven for hours. For two days he'd kept her prisoner in a warehouse. Until Mallory and Cyrus had rescued her.*

She'd never allow anyone to victimize her again. "Who's there?" she shouted. When she got no response, she grabbed a shovel leaning against the shed and pushed her way into the thicket. Whoever had been there was gone now.

Hearing a small pop that had come from the direction of the house, she pushed aside a hibiscus branch to see what it was.

Harry sat down on the back porch steps and took a long pull on a bottle. Heart racing, she ran across the lawn toward the house. "Hey!"

He tipped the bottle at her. "Want a root beer?"

She ignored his offer. "Someone was spying on me."

His gaze fell to the shovel in her hand. Was she accusing him? Standing, he backed away, holding up his free hand in surrender.

Could Jordan be delusional? After all, Harry had caught her conversing with cats yesterday, and now she was acting paranoid, thinking that he was some kind of peeping Tom. Which was a shame, because he'd just started to like her. He'd sworn off relationships for the time being, at least until he knew who he was.

But after he'd met her yesterday, something had shifted inside of him. The sun had shone a little brighter, colors had suddenly appeared more vibrant, and even the food he'd eaten since then tasted better.

Jordan narrowed her eyes at him. "I heard someone sneaking around in the bushes."

"The bushes? I was in the house until a minute ago."

She shook her head. "I wasn't accusing you. I'm just..." She glanced over her shoulder and shivered. "It scared me."

Anger stormed through him. "Tell me exactly what happened."

She tightened the towel around her body. "I felt someone watching me. It's hard to explain. I heard leaves rustling like someone had pushed through. Then footsteps."

"Anything else?"

She shook her head.

He scanned the thick foliage on the far side of the yard. What if the person who'd been messing with him had followed him to the Tuckers' place? Not only could he be in danger, but so could Jordan. "Go inside and lock the door. I'm going to have a look for myself."

She handed him the shovel. "O-okay."

Once she was safely inside the house, he strode the perimeter of the yard. He smelled something unpleasant, like stale smoke, but he couldn't find any evidence that someone had been there. He opened the door to the shed. It was filled with gardening supplies, and none of it appeared to have been disturbed. As Harry took a step into the small, windowless building, his head started pounding. Sweat trickled down the side of his face.

A terrifying memory flashed in his mind—darkness closed in on him. He was in a similar space, so tiny and dark.

Let me out! Please.

Grabbing the door frame, he backed out of the shed and composed himself. Where had the memory come from? Had it merely been an old nightmare, or was it a glimpse into his past? A jail cell? A hidey-hole?

He forced himself to concentrate on the darkness, but as quickly as the image had appeared, it vanished into the locked up hole in his memory.

After another check of the area, he returned to the house and let himself inside. He thought he heard voices, so he stilled.

Not voices—merely one, Jordan's. Sounded as if she was on the phone. Just to be sure, he headed toward her voice. And found her in the study.

She sat on an antique sofa with her back to him. And no phone anywhere to be found. "…How can I stay if I don't feel safe? … Well, that's true. … Are you sure? I knew I hadn't imagined it."

Harry cleared his throat. "Is someone else here?"

Jordan stood up, twisting around to face him. Her cheeks were scarlet. "Um, no. I mean yes." She scrunched her nose in the most adorable way.

"Were you on the phone?" he asked, although he knew that wasn't the case.

"Nope."

"Imaginary friend?"

She wound a platinum blond curl around her index finger and shifted from foot to foot. "I was talking to…"

He folded his arms over his chest as she started to say something then stopped. "Yes?" he ventured.

Her pretty lips flattened to a thin line. "One of the kittens — Tallulah is her name — happened to be looking out the window of one of the upstairs rooms. She saw a man hiding in the bushes a few minutes ago. See? I told you someone was there."

Wow, she really was delusional. "So you're saying that a cat was talking to you?"

Huffing, she sank onto a chair. "It's not exactly like that. But you have to believe me. Tallulah saw a man crouching there,

39

watching me." She glanced toward a black and white kitten and nodded. "And he was smoking a cigar."

A chill rolled over his skin. Yes, what he'd detected near the shed had definitely been cigar smoke. Not that he believed that Jordan had gleaned the snippet of intel from a feline informant. But he was curious enough to play along. "And how could Tallulah have seen a cigar at that distance?"

Jordan rolled her eyes. "Don't you know how much better a cat's vision is than ours? She also said he had red hair."

"Mm-hmm."

"Harry, how long have you lived in Nocturne Falls?"

What did that have to do with anything? "About four years. Why?"

She gave him a wistful nod. "I see. And why did you move here?"

If he tried explaining it to her, she'd think *he* was the crazy one. "It's...a long story."

"Always is." She crossed her legs, giving him a view of her incredibly shapely thighs.

Being a gentleman, he averted his gaze.

"Have you seen many strange things in that time?" she asked.

"Strange?" He wasn't sure what she was getting at but wondered if she was one of those locals who took the whole, Halloween everyday theme as gospel. Did she think that the vampires strolling the town center every evening were real? Or that the gargoyle in the fountain actually turned from flesh and blood to stone at will?

She huffed. "You know what? Never mind. Forget I said anything...about the cats."

Now she was confusing him. "So they don't talk to you?"

She rubbed her temples. "I was a lonely kid, you know? Animals were my only friends. Some kids have imaginary friends. Mine were the four-legged variety."

That didn't explain why she'd insisted that a kitten had seen someone hiding in the bushes. He hadn't misunderstood her. Jordan believed that the cat had spoken to her.

Her phone played a familiar tune. "Excuse me," she said as she answered.

He could only hope the caller was her psychiatrist.

CHAPTER THREE

Jordan crumpled onto the sofa with her cell phone.

"What were you thinking?" Mallory sneezed on the other end of the line.

Every time Jordan tried to do something nice for Mal, she managed to screw it up royally. "I'm sorry." How could she have forgotten that Mallory was allergic to daisies?

"And you didn't sign the note."

Jordan smacked her forehead. "You know my handwriting, Mal. I didn't even consider that Cyrus would be the one to see the bouquet first."

"Well, he did." Mallory sniffled. "Cyrus trusts me a hundred percent, but when he read that, I love you, he wondered if someone was stalking me."

"Again, I'm so sorry. I was only trying to apologize for the kitchen fire." Tears stung behind her eyes.

"Yeah, I know," Mal said. "How's it going there?"

If she told her twin about someone peeping at her through the bushes, Mallory would probably insist that Jordan come back to her house. So much for Mal and Cyrus

42

having that much-needed couple time. Nope, she wouldn't mention it. Besides, the guy was probably long gone by now. "Well, I haven't started a kitchen fire yet. Just give me time." She glanced through the open door into the study at Harry, who was boxing books from the built-in shelves. "It's fine here. Great. The house is a mansion."

"Nice. Glad to hear it."

Jordan nodded. "Mal?"

"Yes?"

"I'm trying to do better."

After several beats, Mallory sighed. "I know you are, hon."

"I love you. And Cyrus."

"Me, too."

A little relieved, Jordan disconnected then returned to the study. "Need help?"

"Sure." He handed her an empty box. "I'll be repairing and refinishing the bookcases soon. This was the quietest task I could think of while you were on the phone."

That was thoughtful of him.

"Everything all right?" he asked. "I wasn't eavesdropping on you, but you looked upset."

She packed books into her box. "It's okay. That was my sister, Mallory. I burned up her kitchen yesterday morning before I left. Then, as an apology, I sent her flowers that she was allergic to. Oh, and I didn't sign the card, so her fiancé thought she had a secret admirer or something."

His eyes opened wide. "Seriously?"

She nodded. "Amazing but true. Story of our relationship. Mal's perfect, and I'm the opposite of perfect."

"How so?"

After lots of recent soul-searching, and many late-night talks with her twin, Jordan had recently gleaned more insight into their childhood, and how it had affected her relationship with Mal. "Mom and Dad were a lot more strict with Mallory than they were with me. They expected more from her because she was smarter, more responsible, harder working than I. Since my standards were lower, I lived up to their expectations by misbehaving. I guess I was trying to get their attention."

He picked up the box Jordan had just finished filling and carried it to the corner where there was already a stack of them. "At least you have a family."

"You don't?"

His expression darkened for a moment. Then he fixed her with a look of pure pity. "You're much more interesting than I am. Animals don't confide in me."

Perhaps she'd told him too much. He probably thought she was mentally ill because she spoke to the cats. Supernaturals in Nocturne Falls weren't supposed to tell non-supes about their gifts, but she felt compelled to prove to Harry that she wasn't making up stories. She didn't imagine that animals spoke to her. Aw, heck. If he lived in Nocturne Falls, he had to be used to strange characters. "I can tell that you don't believe me. I can prove it, though."

He folded his arms over his chest. "Is that right? How would that work?"

"Milo, Rosin," she called out. "Come here, kitties."

A moment later, both felines walked into the study and looked up at her. *What's up?* Milo asked.

We were catnapping, Rosin said.

Harry chuckled. "Lots of cats come when you call them. So does mine."

"That wasn't the proof I was referring to," she said. "I'll go to the other end of the house, or outside if you prefer. Then you tell the cats something."

"Like what?"

She glanced into the box she'd been packing. "How about you pick out a couple of books and read the titles to them? They can tell me which ones you chose. Will that be proof enough?"

He scrubbed a hand over his chin. "It'd be a better test if I gave them random facts."

"Fine."

He poked a finger at her. "And even better if *I* made sure you didn't hear me."

45

"Not a problem."

He crossed the room to the stereo and turned it on. "Have a seat."

She marched over and sat on a leather chair.

Harry raised the volume on the New Orleans-style jazz music. "Just to make sure…" He plugged in a set of headphones, checking them by holding them to his ears. "Perfect."

"Whatever."

Before putting the headphones on her, he tucked her hair behind her ears. The intimate contact sent a pleasant shiver over her skin. The music blared. "Okay, she shouted. I feel like I'm at a concert."

He ushered the cats from the room.

As she waited, she looked out the window. Big, billowy clouds floated past. The news had said it was going to rain today. The forecasters were wrong a lot of the time, though.

Something touched her shoulder. She jumped off the chair, heart pounding.

Harry backed away from her, hands raised in surrender.

Pulling off the headphones, she drew a deep breath to slow her pounding heart. "You scared me."

He shut off the stereo. "Sorry."

"It's okay."

Milo climbed onto the chair Jordan had just vacated and curled up there. Rosin head-bumped Harry's knee.

"What'd Harry tell you, guys?" she asked the cats.

He said he was wearing a flannel shirt and khaki pants when he woke up, Rosin said. *And that he thinks you're pretty.*

Warmth settled in her belly. "Really?"

"What?" Harry asked.

"Hang on a sec." She looked at Milo. "Anything else?"

You have gorgeous hair, Milo said.

And an adorable backside," Rosin added.

Laughing, she faced Harry and took in his cotton work shirt. "You told them you were wearing a flannel shirt and khaki pants. Strange choice for sleepwear."

His face fell.

She moved in closer for the kill. "And thanks for the compliments."

Harry's eyebrows shot higher.

Flipping her hair over her shoulder, she winked at him. "You think I'm pretty, hmm? Particularly my hair…and my backside."

Red-faced, he practically fell into a chair. "How…?"

"Telepathy," she offered. "Sadly, my gift only extends to animals."

Harry remained silent for almost a minute. "I never would have believed it if I hadn't seen it for myself. Can your twin talk to animals, too?"

She shook her head. "Mallory's gift is reading tarot cards. We're both psychic to some degree, just in different ways."

"And your parents?"

"Our powers come from Mom's side."

Pinching the bridge of his nose, he squeezed his eyes shut for a moment. "Forgive me if I'm asking too many questions. I'm trying to get my bearings here. I never imagined that telepathy was real."

That was understandable. She'd blown up the universe as he knew it. He needed time to process that.

When he didn't say anything for several moments, she rubbed her palms together. "I have an idea. I spotted a can of loose-leaf tea in the pantry, the same kind my grandma had. You want some?"

After a moment's hesitation, he shrugged. "Yeah, sure."

In the kitchen, she rummaged through the drawers until she found a mesh tea strainer. She set the old-fashioned kettle on a burner as Harry got two mugs down from a high shelf. Then they sat at the table and waited for the water to boil.

Jordan glanced around the room at the spaces where Harry had already removed most of the cabinets. "You've been busy in here."

"Demolition goes quickly. It's the refurbishment that takes longer." He moved the sugar bowl to the center of the table. "Were you and your twin sister ever close?"

Thinking about the question, she nodded. "We are now. Well, closer than we used to be."

"So you talked to cats because you couldn't confide in her?"

Was he trying to psychoanalyze her? But if that was what it took to draw him out, why not? "You know how books and TV shows have good cop, bad cop scenarios?"

"Sure."

She loaded tea leaves into the strainer then hooked it on the edge of a white ceramic teapot. "Mallory and I played good twin, bad twin."

He laughed. "Okay."

When the kettle whistled, she went to get it. "What about you? Did you have anyone you confided in?" She poured the water into the pot.

"I have no idea. I can't remember anything from my childhood."

Lots of people said that they had no memories before a certain age—usually four or five. She sensed that it was a sensitive subject for him. Could he have experienced a trauma that had caused him to forget his whole early life? Perhaps talking about it would help. "What *do* you remember?"

His lips flattened. "I have no memory at all. Four years ago I woke up in the woods. I had no clue who I was."

She stopped what she was doing. "Seriously? Like you had amnesia?"

"Exactly. I still do. When I told the cats what I was wearing when I woke up, I didn't mean this morning. I was speaking of the clothes I had on when I first came to, four years ago."

Whoa. "Have you tried to find your family?"

He shook his head and poured them each a cup of tea. "I checked a ton of online message boards that list missing persons, but I never found any pictures of myself. I have no clue what my real name is. Harry Hill was something I just adopted."

The poor guy didn't have a past or a family, and she'd been complaining about her sister. She couldn't imagine not having a twin, or parents, or at least, now knowing who they were. Her chest squeezed. "The not knowing would drive me crazy."

"It does. In this case, though, maybe ignorance is bliss." He stirred sugar into his tea. "I was in bad shape when I woke up. I had cuts and bruises, and my clothes were filthy and torn. There's got to be a reason that no one's reported me missing. What if

I'd been in trouble with the law? Maybe the man I used to be was someone better forgotten."

"I doubt that." Anything was possible, though. Sipping her tea, she thought back to the kidnapping last year. The experience had been so terrifying that it had taken her months to trust anyone. And here she was now, alone in a house with a guy who very well could be an escaped convict or a mobster. Or a kidnapper. She gulped then got up and set her cup in the sink. "I think I'm going to read for a while. Or lie down. I'm kind of sleepy." Backing out of the kitchen, she faked a yawn. "See ya."

"Oh, okay. I'll let you know when I'm leaving for the day."

"No, that's all right. I might be napping." With that, she hurried up to her room and locked herself inside. She set her laptop on the bed then dug in her purse for the can of pepper spray she'd started carrying with her since the kidnapping.

Chances were that Harry was just a regular guy, but she couldn't be sure. Soon enough, he'd go home. Until then, she'd hang out with a game of computer solitaire. Better to play it safe and assume the worst about him.

Too bad, because he was kind of cute. With her history of making terrible choices when it came to men, she had no business even considering dating Harry.

Harry packed up his tools at five pm. He hadn't heard a peep from Jordan's room for the past hour. Not that he could blame her for hiding out from him. He'd probably freaked her out by sharing too much about his past, or the lack thereof. Of course, he was pretty freaked out about her powers of telepathy. It wasn't every day you learned that there was such a thing as psychic powers.

Strangely, that knowledge didn't make her any less attractive. On the contrary. Now he knew she wasn't off balance, as he'd suspected. He was more intrigued than he had been before she'd proved herself to him.

Didn't matter. He was in no position to take up with a woman—even a smart, gorgeous one who happened to be telepathic.

Heck, for all he knew, he might have a wife somewhere. Although he hoped not. He hated to think that he might have caused anyone pain, even if it wasn't his fault.

When he'd first arrived in Nocturne Falls, he hadn't been wearing a wedding band, nor did his ring finger bear the indentation or tan line as he'd seen on married people. If he'd had a wife in the past, she'd surely have reported him missing. Even if he was single, he was a man without a past. In good conscience, how could he go out with a woman when he couldn't be sure that he wasn't the sort of man with whom she'd be safe?

He drove the short trip to his house. The second he opened the door, Kitty was all over him, sniffing his boots like a bloodhound. "I promise, I wasn't cheating on you. A bunch of cats live at the house where I'm working." Picking her up, he nuzzled her silky head. "You're the only one for me."

The cat purred loudly.

Harry set her down so he could get her dinner. After he'd filled her bowl, he fixed himself a plate of meatloaf and mashed potatoes left over from the night before. And just as he did most evenings, he sat on his recliner and ate supper in front of the television.

Tonight though, his thoughts kept wandering. He couldn't get Jordan off his mind. From those sparkling blue eyes to her long, silky hair, she was the prettiest woman he'd seen in...as far back as he could remember. And she had a gift he'd never imagined possible. She'd probably be able to have a conversation with his cat.

As if Kitty had known he'd been thinking about her, the cat sat down next to his chair and trilled.

He petted the top of her head. "I wonder what you'd tell me if you could." The feline had been with him since the moment he'd awakened in the woods. And maybe even before then.

Gasping, he set aside his plate and stared down at the cat. If Jordan could communicate with the Tuckers' pets, why not his? The key to his past might have been living in his house, and sleeping at his feet all this time.

He paced the living room, scratching his head. Would it be rude to ask a woman he barely knew to help him figure out his identity? What if he learned that he was a thief, a drug dealer, or worse? Sometimes ignorance was bliss. If he never found out who he was, he could keep living this life he'd made here in Nocturne Falls.

It wasn't so bad. He'd built a successful carpentry business, rented this house, and worked in his garden on his one day off each week. Did he really want to upset that apple cart?

Returning to his chair, he finished his dinner. When he realized he had no idea what he'd just watched on TV, he shut off the set. The more he thought about Jordan's gift, the more the idea grew on him of having her try to speak to Kitty. His pulse raced at the notion of learning who he was.

Thunder rumbled outside. The lights flickered. Would Jordan be nervous all alone in a strange house? He considered driving over there to check on her. If he did, he could also run his idea past her of having her pick his cat's brain. With a glance at the clock, he realized it was too late to just show up at the Tuckers' place unannounced. That would surely frighten her. Too bad he didn't have her number. But she had a business, so she was probably listed online.

It only took him a minute to locate Jordan's pet sitting company's Facebook page. He tried her number and went to voicemail. She'd probably gone to bed by now.

Somehow, he'd have to wait until morning to speak with her. He had no doubt that he wouldn't be able to sleep, not with the prospect of finding out who he was so close at hand.

CHAPTER FOUR

As Jordan changed into her pajamas, she wondered if she'd made a mistake by telling Harry about her gift. There was an unspoken policy in the town of keeping the non-supes blissfully ignorant of the fact that so many of the residents weren't completely human, or at least had supernatural powers. As long as Harry didn't go blabbing what he now knew to other normies, it should be okay.

The door to her room creaked open. She sucked in a breath but relaxed when Theo pushed through. "You scared me, Theo."

Sorry. The tabby jumped onto the window seat. *I want a treat.*

Stepping into her bunny slippers, Jordan grabbed her cell. "Okay, come on." On the way to the kitchen, she noticed a missed call on her phone, which reminded her that the battery was super low. She couldn't remember where she'd stashed her charger, but she'd find it after she got the cat his treat.

Theo weaved in front of her, making sure that she didn't go anywhere except the kitchen. Milo, Rosin, and Rorschach joined the procession, all meowing at her.

We want some, too, Rorschach implored.

"You have to let me walk, guys," she told them.

After giving each cat a few treats, she searched the freezer until she found a pint of ice cream. Mrs. Tucker had told her to help herself to the food they'd left, so she fixed herself a sundae then headed to the study. The only interesting thing she could find on TV was an old vampire flick. So she settled into the velvet sofa with the cats to watch it. On the screen, Bela Lugosi dramatically descended a gothic-looking staircase.

Milo kept trying to steal a bite of her ice cream.

"Quit that." She moved it out of his reach. "You already had yours."

Outside, the wind howled. Lightning flashed, illuminating the darkened room. Something scraped against the house. All the cats sat up in unison.

"It's only the storm," she assured them. Growing up in south Florida with frequent hurricanes had given her a healthy fear of mother nature. A boom of thunder rattled the windows. The power went out. Riding out a bad storm alone in a strange house in the dark seemed about as much fun as being waterboarded. Jordan waited, offering up a prayer that the lights would come back on.

A distant memory came to mind.

She and Mallory were only four or five years old. A terrible storm raged outside. They'd lost power. Everything was pitch black and as loud as a train. Jordan held her hands over her ears. "I'm scared, Mal," Jordan cried.

"Mallory," their mother shouted. "Where are you?"

Jordan waited for their mom to call her name.

"Take my hand," Mom said.

Jordan reached for her twin.

"Good girl." Their mom picked up Mallory and started down the stairs.

"Mommy!" Jordan shrieked. "Don't leave me."

"I'll come back for you," she shouted. "I promise."

Jordan curled up in a ball. Minutes felt like hours as she waited, alone, terrified, abandoned.

Years later, when she'd asked her mother why she'd taken Mallory first that night—why Mal always seemed to come before Jordan—her mom had waved off the question. But Jordan knew. Mallory was their parents' golden child, Miss Perfect. And the reason they let Jordan get away with everything. Each time Jordan pushed the envelope, disobeyed their rules, they never punished her because they expected less from her.

She shook off the memory.

"Where do they keep the flashlights and candles?" she asked the cats.

In a kitchen drawer, Rosin supplied.

She hadn't remembered to charge her phone. Darn it! Hoping for the best, she turned on the flashlight app. After only a moment her cell died. She couldn't see a thing as she made her way toward the kitchen.

Watch out, Rorschach warned.

Too late. She stubbed her toe on a furniture leg. The pain stopped her in her tracks. "Ouchie!"

A blue streak lit up the room for a split second. Out of the corner of her eye, Jordan could have sworn that she saw a shadow move past the window, one that looked like a person. A chill slithered up her spine.

Only my imagination, she assured herself. Still, her heart pounded against her ribs. She limped the rest of the way to the kitchen and frantically pulled open drawers, searching for a flashlight.

Somebody's outside, Theo told her. *A stranger.*

Jordan gasped. The terrifying memory of her kidnapping flashed through her mind.

Glass shattered nearby. Then someone jiggled the kitchen doorknob.

She stifled a scream. Her legs felt leaden, but she forced herself to move. Quietly as she could, she hurried from the room. Why had she left her pepper spray upstairs in her purse? It was all she could think of to protect herself. When she was halfway up the staircase, she heard the distinctive creak of the floorboards in the foyer.

Her blood ran hot with panic. The intruder was there, less than ten feet away. All she could hear was the thump, thump, thump of her heartbeat. Finally, she made it to her room and locked herself inside. Fishing in her purse, she closed her trembling fingers around the can of pepper spray.

The intruder tried her doorknob.

Oh, God, oh, God.

Harry pulled his hood over his head before getting out of his truck and running through the storm to the porch of the Tucker house. The power was out all over the area, so he felt compelled to check on Jordan. He knocked, but after she didn't answer, decided to use his key. In the foyer, a strange feeling sent a shiver over his skin. "Jordan?" he called. "It's Harry."

"Harry!" she shouted from somewhere upstairs. "Be careful. Someone's broken in."

Every nerve and muscle in his body was instantly on high alert. "Don't say another word," he called to Jordan. Whoever was in the house could follow her voice to her location. He had to get the intruder to come to him and leave Jordan alone.

Reaching into his pocket, he pulled out his phone and dialed 911. But before he could hit Send, a powerful blow to the back of his head stopped him cold. Stars swam before his eyes. He couldn't pass out. Jordan needed him. Struggling to maintain consciousness, he spun around to face his attacker. He tried to make out the man's face, but all he could see was the whites of his eyes.

Suddenly, the silence shattered with what sounded like dozens of cats growling and hissing. The intruder backed away from Harry as a hoard of cats attacked him. A flash of lightning briefly illuminated the scene. The man flailed his arms in an attempt to get them off. *"Slez ze mě!"*

Harry hung onto the banister, desperately trying to ward off the fog creeping into his brain. He managed to send the emergency call as the edges of his field of vision shrank.

"Nine-one-one," the operator said. "What's your emergency?"

The burglar gasped. He yanked open the front door and charged through the threshold, landing on all fours on the porch. "Get off!" he shouted at the cats in heavily accented English.

The cats didn't relent until the man rolled off the porch. Then they ran back into the house and scattered. Harry managed to kick shut the door. "Jordan, he's gone," he called over his shoulder.

A door opened upstairs. Rapid footsteps descended the steps.

"Harry! My God, are you all right?" Jordan crouched next to him and cradled his head in her lap.

He smiled up at her. "I am now."

"Nine-one-one," the voice on the other end of the line said again.

Jordan picked up his phone. "We need police and medical help at 407 Eerie Avenue."

Harry kept fighting the haze in his head that threatened to pull him under. He closed his eyes for a moment.

"Mr. Hill?" someone said. "Can you hear me?" It was a woman, but not Jordan.

Harry blinked his eyes open then immediately closed them again against the overhead lights. A policewoman stood over him. "Yes," he said. "Is Jordan okay?"

The officer nodded. "She's right here."

Jordan's pretty face replaced the cop's, her eyes glistening. "I'm fine."

"Medical's here," the officer said.

"What do we have?" a uniformed man asked.

"Mr. Hill was unconscious for a minute or two," the policewoman told the man.

"I'm Aiden," the man said. "I'm an EMT. Can you tell me what happened to you?"

Harry told them about the intruder, and when he'd finished, the EMT asked if Harry wanted to go to the hospital.

"You should be checked out by a doctor," Aiden said.

Harry sat up. "That's not necessary."

"Head trauma can be tricky." Aiden frowned. "You're taking a big chance by refusing care. But I can't force you to go."

Harry gave him a thumbs up. "Got it. I'm okay, really."

"It's not a good idea for you to be alone tonight."

Jordan touched the EMT's arm. "He won't be alone, Aiden. I'll stay with him."

Was she serious? Harry met Jordan's stare. She gave him a half nod.

Aiden's brow shot higher on his forehead. "Oh, okay."

"Thanks, Aiden," Jordan told the man. "Give Darcy a hug for me."

After the EMTs left, Jordan took Harry into the living room. "Why don't you relax on the sofa. Hopefully, the police will finish up soon."

Harry heard the two officers talking in the kitchen, but he couldn't make out what they were saying. "What are they doing?" he asked Jordan.

"Taking fingerprints, I think." She sat next to him and handed him an ice pack.

"You don't have to babysit me," he told her as he held the icepack against the bump on the back of his head. "I'll be okay to go home soon."

She rolled her eyes toward the heavens. "I don't think so. Besides, what makes you think I want to be here all alone? There's safety in numbers."

She had a point. The more Harry thought about it, he knew he couldn't leave her there. "We can go to my place tonight."

Her lips bunched to one side, but she remained silent.

He replayed the events of the evening. "Did you have anything to do with the cats attacking the guy who broke in?"

Her gaze darted around the room. "Maybe."

"If you did orchestrate that...well, thanks."

"Don't mention it." She glanced toward the kitchen then slid closer to him and lowered her voice. "So you totally believe in my gift now, hmm?"

He'd have never guessed that anyone could communicate telepathically, let alone do it with animals. But Jordan had proven herself twice, and one of those instances had probably saved Harry's life. "A hundred percent."

A big smile made her even prettier. Even in whimsical pajamas with a dog and cat pattern, and ridiculously huge bunny slippers, she was gorgeous. She wore not a stitch of make-up, yet her skin looked peaches-and-cream fresh.

The male deputy came into the living room and introduced himself as Deputy Cruz. "We weren't able to get any good prints from the doorknob," he said. "Do you remember if the perpetrator wore gloves?"

"I never saw him," Jordan replied.

Harry thought back to his fight with the intruder. "It was dark. I'm not sure." He set the icepack in a crystal bowl on the coffee table. "He had an accent."

Cruz raised a dark eyebrow. "What kind of accent?"

He replayed the scene in his head. "Maybe Slavic. Something eastern European."

The deputy wrote on a tablet computer. "There'll be an officer patrolling the neighborhood tonight. If you need anything, please let us know."

"Oh!" Jordan held her hand over her mouth for a moment.

"What is it?" the cop asked.

"I wonder if the guy who broke in could have been the same man who was watching me from the bushes." She explained what had happened when she'd been sunbathing.

The officer's eyes shifted from brown to dark gold, and then back again.

Harry rubbed the bridge of his nose. Maybe his eyesight had been affected by the knock on his head.

"But you never actually saw the man?" the officer asked.

"No, only one of the cats did."

The cop absently nodded, as if Jordan hadn't told him something unbelievable. Was the police force in on Jordan's supernatural gift?

The deputy shook hands with Jordan and then Harry. "Please don't hesitate to call if you think of anything else."

"Thank you, Deputy Cruz," Jordan said. "We will."

After the cops left, Harry locked the doors. Seeing the broken window in the back door, he mumbled a curse under his breath." The best I can do to fix this tonight is to nail a piece of plywood over it. First thing in the morning, I'll hit the DIY Depot for the glass."

"You think we'll be okay here tonight?" Jordan hugged her arms around her body. Her furrowed brow was the first evidence he'd noticed that the break-in had taken its toll on her.

Something inside him twisted with anger. "I promise you that I'll protect you. If you'd rather go to my place, though, that's fine with me."

She bit her bottom lip, and Harry couldn't help but find the gesture sexy. She cut those clear, blue eyes at him and he nearly came apart at the seams. He couldn't remember the last time he'd kissed a woman, but he knew that she'd be the next and that it would be amazing.

He had to stay sharp, though. Getting sucked under by Jordan's charms would only distract him from his mission to keep her safe.

"I wouldn't feel right leaving the cats tonight," she said. "They've been through trauma as sure as you and I have."

"Sure. I'll camp out on the sofa if that's all right with you."

"There's another guest room upstairs."

"This is fine—more stategic."

Her smile widened for a moment. "Okay. I'll grab you a blanket and pillow from upstairs."

When Jordan left the room, Harry went out to his truck for his tools and some scrap plywood. As he climbed the porch steps, he took the opportunity to scan the area. Under cover of darkness, the street appeared idyllic and safe. Now he knew better.

Back in the kitchen a few minutes later, he nailed a board over the broken window then reinforced it with two by fours.

"Let's hope that does it," Jordan said from behind him.

Showing her his hammer, he said, "No one will get past me."

"I'm sure that's true." New lines creased her forehead. She rubbed her eyes. "I'm wiped out. I guess I'll go upstairs. You probably want to get to sleep, too."

Not likely. "Are you sure you're okay?"

She shrugged. "I will be."

After she'd gone to bed, Harry settled into the sofa, but he refused to go to sleep. The events of the evening buzzed through his head. Too many questions remained unanswered: What had the intruder been after? Could it have been the person who'd stolen Harry's mail and broken into his truck?

A floorboard creaked, galvanizing his attention. "Jordan?" he ventured as he grabbed his hammer from the coffee table.

"It's just me," she called from the foyer.

Most of the tension in his neck and shoulders released. "Are you all right?"

Still wearing those adorably silly bunny slippers, she padded into the room, followed by two cats. "Can't sleep." She picked up the black and white spotted kitten and nuzzled its head. "Rorschach had no problem snoozing. She snores."

"How about some tea?"

The orange tabby at Jordan's feet meowed up at him.

"And a treat for you," Harry told the cat.

Jordan batted her eyelashes. "Perhaps something stronger, eh? I spotted an open bottle of wine in the fridge. By the time the Tuckers get back here, it'll be no good. We might as well polish it off."

After getting knocked out earlier, he doubted he ought to be drinking. Plus, he needed to keep a clear head just in case his attacker came back. "You go ahead. I'll get myself a glass of water."

She gestured for him to stay where he was. "I'll bring it to you. Be right back."

He tried to ignore how the sexy sway of her backside as she left the room.

"Do you take ice in your water?" Jordan called from the kitchen.

"Sure." Hopefully, that would cool him down, although what he needed was a cold shower. Being alone with Jordan all night was dangerous on so many levels. The more he cared about her, the less he could chance starting something with her.

"Here we are," she said as she returned and handed him the drink. She tapped her wineglass to his water glass. "Cheers."

"To what are we toasting?"

"Surviving the break-in tonight." She bowed. "And thank you again for coming to my rescue."

"Glad to help." He didn't want to think about what could have happened to her had he not been there.

"What brought you over here?"

"It's hard to explain." He scrubbed a hand over his face and considered her question. "I got this idea while I was eating dinner..." But now wasn't the time to lay his problems on her shoulders, or ask her for help in finding out whatever he could about his past. "Anyway, I was going to wait until morning to speak to you about something. A little while after it started storming, I lost power at my place, which is close to here. I figured that the electricity was out here, you might be scared of being in a strange house."

Her blue eyes sparkled as she sat next to him. "That was sweet of you. Part of the whole being-responsible-for-me-because-you-saved-my-life thing?"

"I guess."

She fluttered her eyelashes. "I don't know what I'd have done if you hadn't shown up." Her gaze fell to his mouth.

His pulse kicked up several notches. Their lips were mere inches apart. God, he wanted to kiss her. Taking a lock of her hair between his fingers, he looked deep into her eyes and saw his desire mirrored there.

He inhaled her sweet, coconut scent. But he shouldn't. He couldn't.

CHAPTER FIVE

Had Jordan imagined Harry's interest in her? Why had he backed away? Maybe he was one of those rare, chivalrous men who liked to ask a girl first before they kissed her. Her answer was yes, yes, yes.

Right now she didn't care about her history of choosing the wrong guys. Harry had come to her rescue twice now, and tonight he'd put his life on the line for her. That had to count for something.

The notion that they both could have died a few hours ago made her want to take a bigger bite out of life. She didn't want some long, involved relationship, but she couldn't deny that she found Harry incredibly attractive. They were here now, and in a few weeks, they'd disappear from each other's lives. She was lonely. And he was so darn sexy.

She set down her drink and scootched a smidge closer.

His lips flattened. "Jordan," he started.

She silenced him with a kiss. Heart kabooming, she plowed her fingers through his thick hair. He tasted of mint and desire.

Wrapping his arms around her, he drew her against the muscled hardness of his chest.

Yes, this was exactly what she'd hoped for — that safe, secure sensation, as if nothing could hurt her as long as she was in his arms. As long as she remembered that it was temporary, it'd be fine.

Harry trailed his tongue around the shell of her ear, inciting a flood of desire, and turning her into a puddle of a woman.

She leaned back on the sofa, stretching out on the cushion, and crooked her finger at him to join her.

Wearing a lusty grin, he complied. He propped himself up on one elbow and trailed his hand over her side.

Everything fell away. There was only the moment, the two of them, drunk on their rising passion. She had no idea what time it was when they finally came up for air, but a sliver of orange light poked through the curtains.

Harry smoothed her hair off her cheek then kissed the tip of her nose. "I've got a confession."

Was he going to tell her something about himself that would put him in her poor-choices-in-men category? Swallowing, she eased herself up. "What is it?"

He sat against the opposite arm. "Checking that you were okay in the blackout wasn't the only reason I came here tonight."

A little while earlier, he'd started to tell her that he had to discuss something with her. She steeled herself for a letdown. "Okay."

Lines fanned out from the corners of his eyes. "You remember what I said about not remembering my past?"

"Sure."

"There might be a way you can help me with that."

"Me?"

Taking her hand, he nodded. "If you don't want to do it, I completely understand. No pressure."

Now he'd piqued her curiosity. "All right."

He drew a deep breath before speaking. "When I woke up without my memory, I was in the woods, not far from the highway. I was banged up and bruised. And I had no identification on me—no wallet, nothing. This white cat was there with me. For a long time, I'd assumed that she'd been a stray, and had just wandered upon me." He reached to the coffee table for his glass and took a sip of water. "She's still with me. I call her Kitty."

"How original," she teased.

Some of the tension in his expression eased. "After you showed me your gift, I got an idea. It's a longshot, I know."

Now she understood where he was going with this. "So you want me to ask your cat if she saw anything, if she was with you before you woke up."

Harry nodded. "You don't have to decide now. Take your time. Think about it."

Of course, she'd do it. Why wouldn't she use her powers to help the man who'd risked his life for her? The ring of her cell phone startled her. Who'd be calling this early? "I should get that."

"Sure, go ahead."

She disengaged herself from him and hurried to the kitchen, where she'd left her phone. By the time she picked it up, the caller had hung up. Checking the display, she saw her dad's name. Her stomach churned. According to her cell, it was a few minutes after six in the morning, way earlier than he'd ever called before. "That was my father," she told Harry. "I've got to call him back."

He gave her a thumbs up.

Her dad answered on the second ring. "Hi sweetheart," he said. "I hope my call didn't wake you."

"No, I was up. Is everything okay?"

"Fine. I've got exciting news."

"What's that?"

"Mom and I will be passing through Nocturne Falls on our way to your aunt's place in Chattanooga. We'd like to take you and your sister to lunch."

That was a relief. "Great. When are you coming?"

"Today. Barring any traffic problem, we should arrive at about noon. We're half an hour past Macon."

What? "Why didn't you give us more notice? Does Mal know?"

"I called her before I did you."

Of course, he did.

"We're looking forward to meeting her future husband."

Her mom said something in the background, but Jordan couldn't make it out.

"I'll ask her, Carol," her dad said to her mother. "Mom wants to know if you're dating anyone."

All the insecurities from her childhood crept out from beneath the rock where she kept them hidden. "S-sure I am."

"Invite him to join us," her father said.

Oops. "I think he's already got plans," Jordan told him.

"This is a special occasion, Jordan. If your sister and her fiance can make it, so can your boyfriend. We won't take no for an answer."

She racked her brain for an excuse to get her imaginary boyfriend off the hook.

Harry came into the kitchen and refilled his water glass.

Which gave Jordan an idea. With Harry standing at the sink with his back to her, Jordan seized the opportunity to check out his rear view, which was almost as great as his front. "Um, I'll do my best."

"Make sure you do," her dad said. "I'll text you the details. We'll see you in a few hours."

She disconnected and stuck her phone in the pocket of her pajama pants. Her mouth was dry as sand as she turned on the coffee maker.

"You okay?" Harry drained his water glass.

"Fine." She tried for a smile. "That was my dad. He and Mom are coming up from Miami today on their way to my aunt's house in Tennessee."

"That's nice."

No, it wasn't. Had they purposely chosen not to give her any notice of their visit? Rubbing her temples to ward off the first pangs of a headache, she sighed.

"You don't want to see them?" Harry asked.

"I do. I love my family." She sank onto a kitchen chair. "It's just that being with them usually feels like a test; as if they're waiting for me to say something wrong, or to mess up somehow."

Harry joined her at the table. "Is there anything I can do?"

God, she hated to ask him to pretend to be her boyfriend. He'd already done so much for her. "Well…"

"What?"

"Dad asked if I'd bring…a date." She got up to fetch a cup of coffee. "Want one?" she asked Harry.

"Okay." He got the cream out of the fridge and set it on the table. "So what's the problem?"

"I said that I have a boyfriend. I don't know why it matters to me what they think. Mallory's engaged to this wonderful guy." She huffed. "Would you pretend to be my date?"

Frowning, Harry took one of the mugs from her. "I can't do that."

Her mood clunked. Had their make-out session been nothing more than killing time for him? "Um…okay."

He closed the distance between them. "I don't want to pretend. I'll be your *real* date."

The knots in her gut relaxed. And as she looked into Harry's eyes, the flame of her desire reignited. "Yeah?"

He took her hand. "I'd be honored."

"Thank you."Lifting on her tiptoes, she kissed his cheek. "And my answer is yes, too. I'd be happy to have a conversation with your cat."

Rolling his eyes, he said, "Wow."

"What?" she asked.

"Just unpacking that sentence. You'll have a conversation with my cat. Twenty-four hours ago I thought..." His lips flattened to a thin line.

"That I was crazy?" she supplied.

His silence confirmed it.

"It's okay," she said. "I get it."

"What time is lunch?"

She checked her phone and found a long text from her father. "Noon," she told Harry. "My sister suggested Mummy's. Have you been there?"

He nodded. "Sure. Good hamburgers and their pies are out of this world."

"Definitely." And the service at Mummy's was usually fast. Less time for her parents to ask too many probing questions about her 'boyfriend,' or the solvency of her business. But she had no time to waste. "I still have to walk a couple of dogs this morning. I'd better get myself together." She started from the room.

"Can I meet you at the diner?" Harry asked. "I've still got to pick up a glass pane at the DIY Depot, and I'd like to stop at my house after to change my clothes."

"Yeah, that'll work."

"Hey," Harry called to her.

Stopping, she turned to face him. "Hmm?"

He crooked his finger at her and grinned.

Heat washed over her as she neared him.

Harry drew her against him for a passionate kiss. Then he stroked his fingers over her jaw. "That's better."

It sure was.

Jordan showered and dressed. She couldn't keep her thoughts off of Harry, replaying their kisses in her mind's eye. Each memory brought a flutter to her heart. She'd chosen her favorite jeans with Harry in mind—because they looked good on her, and her *Pampered Pets* T-shirt for her parents—so they'd know she was doing her best to build her business.

Before she left, she found Harry and indulged in one more kiss.

With an appreciative whistle, he trailed his eyes over her body. "Nice jeans."

"Thanks." She slung her handbag over her shoulder. "Mummy's Diner at noon."

"I'll be there."

As she drove to her first client's house, she couldn't keep the smile off of her face. Even the prospect of walking one of her least favorite dogs couldn't ruin her mood. Charlemagne, the normally-morose beagle whose owner was a high-powered lawyer who worked long days, did his business in record time.

Jordan let him back inside the house and unhooked his leash. "Thank you,

Charlemagne. You deserve a reward for that."

The dog wagged his tail. *Give me one of the treats you carry*, he told Jordan. *I don't like the ones my human buys.*

"Deal."

After she'd finished taking care of the Peppermans' two Siamese cats, she got in her car and checked her hair in the rearview mirror. She'd be a few minutes early for lunch if she left now, which might impress her folks a little since Mallory was the more punctual twin. But that was in the past. Jordan desperately wanted to show them the new and improved version of herself.

She parked at the restaurant, glancing around for Harry's truck, which she didn't see. Standing near the doorway to the diner, she glimpsed Mallory and Cyrus with her parents. No wonder Jordan never managed to make it anywhere before they did.

No, she wouldn't fall into that old patterns of feeling as if she could never do anything right. She was doing so much better—or at least, she was trying. Checking her lip-gloss and her hair once more, she drew a deep breath then headed over to the entrance.

"There she is!" Her mother split the distance between them and pulled Jordan into a hug.

Jordan inhaled the familiar scent of her mom's vanilla perfume. "Hi, Mom."

"Let me look at you." Holding Jordan at arm's length, she gave her the once-over. "You're too skinny, sweetheart."

Her dad nodded his agreement. "And you're pale. A little sunshine never hurt anyone."

Jordan's heart fell. They hadn't even noticed her T-shirt.

Mallory—the picture of perfection in a sunny yellow dress—greeted her with a kiss on the cheek. "You look fine," her twin whispered in her ear. "Don't let them get to you."

Easy for Mal to say, but Jordan appreciated her sister's comment. "Thanks."

Cyrus hung back and smiled at her, probably still irritated with her over the kitchen fire.

"Where's this boyfriend of yours?" her father asked.

Thankfully, Mallory held her tongue and didn't question Jordan about the mystery man's identity.

"He's meeting us here," Jordan replied.

They all went inside.

Mallory excused herself to go to the restroom.

As they waited for a table, a middle-aged brunette approached Jordan and pulled her into a hug. "Hey, how are you? Is this your family?" Before Jordan could ask who she was, the woman started signing Mallory's praises to their parents. "You must be so proud. Mallory is such a delight and a fabulous manicurist. I was so happy for her when she bought her house last year. And soon she's getting married." The woman patted Cyrus's arm. "I've heard so much about you," she told him. "Congratulations, lovebirds."

Cyrus shook his head. "This isn't —"

"No need to be humble," the brunette interrupted. "I've heard all about your success in real estate. Mallory brags on you all the time."

Jordan wished the black and white checkered floor would open up and swallow her. Sure, Mallory was an impressive young woman, but Jordan had been trying to make her life a success, too.

"How many?" A waitress picked up several menus and packets of silverware.

"Six," Jordan immediately answered.

"I'll let you all go," the middle-aged woman said. "See you next week, Mallory."

Rather than set the lady straight, Jordan gave her a thumbs up.

The waitress seated them at a large, red vinyl booth, and handed them each a menu. "I'll give you a minute," she said, then walked away.

Mallory finally returned and slid in next to her fiance.

Cyrus set down his menu. "I knew what I was ordering before we got here. Their burgers and cheese fries are legendary. And I highly recommend the strawberry milkshakes."

"Yeah, if you have a supersonic metabolism." Mallory shook her head. "I'm going to get the chef salad."

Jordan checked her phone. Harry was only a few minutes late. She had confidence he'd show up any moment.

"Does your boyfriend have a name, Jordan?" her father asked.

Mallory raised an eyebrow at Jordan, who gave her twin a super-quick smile.

Thanks for not ratting me out, sister.

"Harry," Jordan said.

"Are y'all ready to order?" Their waitress fished out an order pad and a pen.

Their mom checked her watch. "We don't have much time, Jordan. Are you sure your boyfriend is coming?"

"He said he was." If he didn't make it, not only would Jordan's family think she was a failure, but also a liar.

"Why don't you order for Harry?" her mom suggested,

Gulping, Jordan scanned the menu. "Come back to me, please," she told the waitress.

After the others had given their orders, Jordan glanced at the door, praying that Harry would walk through. When he didn't, an ache started at her temples.

Harry had already come to her rescue twice. Perhaps she'd used up her quota of saves. "I'll start with a strawberry milkshake," she told the waitress. She needed something sweet to wash away the bitter taste of disappointment.

CHAPTER SIX

Someone was following him.

Harry checked his rearview mirror again. The black Buick had dropped back several car lengths, but even after Harry had made a series of roundabout turns, the sedan was still there.

What the hell was going on? Why would anyone follow him? What could they want? There was only one way to find out. Steeling himself to confront the person, Harry pulled to the curb.

The Buick slowed way down as it passed then sped off. Unfortunately, the dark tinted windows had made it impossible for him to see the driver.

Harry clenched his jaw as he pulled out onto the road. The other vehicle weaved around cars then made a left turn from the right lane, nearly hitting a grey-haired woman crossing the street.

The elderly woman let go of her walker to clutch her chest.

Was she all right?

Harry punched the steering wheel. He couldn't just leave a helpless and possibly traumatized lady there, so he parked his truck and got out to check on her.

His gut told him he'd just lost an opportunity to learn the identity of the man who'd broken into the Tuckers' house last night, but right now his biggest concern was the octogenarian. He ran across the street to her. "Are you okay, ma'am?"

"What's that?" she asked.

"Are you hurt," he said a little louder.

"No, I don't think so."

He led her to a bench where she sat down and took several deep breaths. "That black car almost ran me over. What a jerk."

"Did you happen to get a look at him?"

"Book him?" She scrunched her forehead. "I'm not sure what that means."

"The man in the car," he repeated. "Were you able to see what he looked like?"

She shook her head. "It happened too fast."

"I can take you to the hospital," he offered.

Waving away his concern, she said, "That's not necessary. You're a dear for asking."

If he had a grandmother or mother somewhere out there, he hoped people were kind to her. "Can I give you a lift anywhere?"

"You're a nice man. I live a couple of blocks away. A ride would be lovely." She patted his arm. "Your wife or girlfriend is lucky to have you."

Her comment reminded him that he was supposed to be meeting Jordan and her family. "Excuse me," he told the woman. "I've got to make a call." He stepped a few yards away to phone Jordan but went straight to voicemail. After leaving her an apologetic message, he helped the old woman to his car then drove her home.

The good deed took longer than he'd hoped. His senior passenger — who introduced herself as Mrs. Reed, insisted Harry come inside.

A chihuahua met them in the front hall, yapping like crazy.

"It's okay, Mambo," Mrs. Reed told the pooch.

"Hush, Mambo," a man said from another room.

When the man came into the foyer, Harry recognized him as the EMT who'd shown up at the Tuckers' house after the break-in. "Whoa," Harry said. "Small world. You live here?"

"Next door. This is my grandmother. What are *you* doing here?" Aiden looked from her to Harry. "Are you all right, Grandma?"

"All night? I've only been gone a little while."

Aiden scrubbed a hand over his face. "You forgot to put in your hearing aids, Grandma. I asked if you were okay."

Mrs. Reed sat on an upholstered bench. "Thanks to this young man, I am. Some maniac driver nearly killed me."

"I just gave her a lift home," Harry said.

"I appreciate that." Aiden shook hands with him.

Mrs. Reed told Aiden about the speeding sedan, and Harry helping her across the street. Then she pulled herself up with her walker. "At least let me send you off with some of my world-famous butterscotch fudge. I've got a fresh batch in the fridge."

Harry backed toward the door. "Actually, I've got to run. I'm late for...an appointment."

Mrs. Reed narrowed her eyes at Harry. "You say you're getting anointed?"

Aiden and Harry laughed.

"I'll explain after you put in your hearing aids," Aiden told her. Then he walked Harry out. "I owe you one, man."

"Not at all. She's a sweet lady."

By the time Harry arrived at Mummy's, he spotted Jordan in a corner booth with four other people. A waitress was clearing away their dishes. Darn it. He'd let Jordan down. Before he went over to apologize, he paid their tab. That done, he headed to their table. For a split second, he thought he saw double until he remembered that Jordan and her twin were identical. With a second glance, he was able to tell them apart. Mallory exuded confidence that Jordan didn't possess.

The sisters sat on either side of a very tall, dark-haired man. The twins' parents occupied the other side of the booth. The resemblance between mother and daughters was uncanny—same blue, cat-shaped eyes, same blond hair, although their mother's was cut short. Their father had salt-and-pepper hair and was fitter than Harry would have expected for a man who appeared to be in his late fifties. His expression was serious but not unkind.

Jordan's face lit up when she saw him. His pulse quickened. "I'm so sorry I'm late."

The older man frowned at him, but the younger one stood up and shook hands with Harry. "Cyrus Barker," he said. "Nice to meet you."

"Harry Hill." Next, he offered his hand to Jordan's father, who hesitated a moment before shaking with him.

"Glad you finally made it," Jordan's dad said. "I'm Tom, and this is my wife, Carol."

After the rest of the introductions, Harry slid into the booth next to Jordan. "I'm sorry I let you down," he whispered against her ear. "I'll explain later."

She squeezed his hand under the table. "I'm just glad you're here now."

"I tried to call."

Jordan rifled in her purse. "Oh, jeez. I must have left my phone in my car."

"Miss," Tom said to the waitress as she cleared the rest of the dishes away. "Can I have our check, please?"

"It's already taken care of." The waitress tipped her chin toward Harry. "He paid it while y'all weren't looking."

"What?" Carol gave Harry a warm smile. "You shouldn't have."

"It was the least I could do after I was so late."

Jordan hooked Harry's arm as the group left the restaurant. "That was so sweet. And stealthy."

In the parking lot, Carol and Tom hugged their daughters goodbye.

Tom shook hands with Cyrus and then Harry. "I hope we'll see you boys next time we come through Nocturne Falls," he said.

"Absolutely," Cyrus replied.

Harry nodded his agreement. Although he'd only known Jordan a couple of days, he liked her. A lot. Which gave him more urgent and personal reasons to find out his identity. Without knowing his past, he didn't dare even consider embarking on a future.

He offered up a wish that his cat held the key to who he was. With any luck, soon he'd know his past, and wouldn't have to hold back his desire for Jordan.

Walking through downtown, hand-in-hand with Harry, Jordan wondered if she should pinch herself. Was he too good to be true? Sure, they'd only pretended to be a real couple for her family, yet something told her that Harry was different from the other guys she'd dated.

For one thing, he wasn't a jerk. Quite the contrary. He'd come through for her again and again and had asked nothing of her.

She paused under a green striped awning to look in the window of Bell, Book & Candle, the local bookstore, but Harry kept walking until their fingers pulled apart.

"Oh, sorry," he said. "I guess I was zoning out."

"Are you okay?"

He scrubbed a hand over his chin but didn't answer.

"Harry?" she prodded.

"Hmm?" His smile didn't reach his eyes.

Jordan led him to a nearby bench. "What's going on? You seem totally distracted."

His lips compressed. "Yeah, I am."

Sliding closer on the bench, she touched his arm. "Does this have anything to do with why you were so late for lunch?"

Tiny muscles ticked around his jaw. "On my way to the restaurant, I noticed a black car following me."

Her heart sped up. "You think it was the guy who broke into the house last night?"

"That'd be my first guess." New lines fanned out from the corners of his eyes. "I pulled over, hoping he'd stop, too. That strategy didn't work. He almost ran over an elderly woman crossing the street."

"Geez."

"Yeah. Which is why I was late. I ended up taking the woman home. She's your friend Aiden's grandmother, and she's fine now."

That was sweet of him. "I know Mrs. Reed. She's a client at the Hair Scare, where Mallory works."

He rubbed the bridge of his nose. "I wonder if the driver of that car is someone from my past. Maybe I did him wrong, or hurt someone he cares about."

The uncertainty and worry in his expression cut straight through her. "I doubt you were the kind of person who would have done that."

Harry drew his hands into fists. "I'd like to believe that, but I can't be sure."

"Look," Jordan said. "The core of who you are likely didn't change just because you lost your memory. You're a good guy. You probably always were."

He frowned. "There's something I need to tell you."

She swallowed hard. "What?"

"My car was broken into last week, and my mailbox a couple days before that." He took her hand in his. "I don't want to put you in danger, Jordan. That man could have hurt you last night." He shuddered. "If I hadn't shown up when I had —"

"But you did." His admission gave her pause. Clearly, the intruder was a dangerous man.

"This could all be connected."

And Harry could be the one in danger. A chill rolled over her skin. She'd just found him. The prospect of losing him — of never getting the opportunity to see where things between them might lead — tied her up in knots. "There's got to be something we can do."

He met her stare. "I have an idea. It's a longshot, though."

"A longshot's better than nothing."

He nodded. "If you don't want to do it, I'll understand."

"I'll help any way I can." A cool breeze whipped her hair around her face.

Harry smoothed a stray strand off of her cheek. "I told you about my cat."

"Kitty."

"Right. She was there with me when I woke up in the woods without any memory." He waited as a young couple strode past. "I've always assumed that the cat had merely happened upon me that day as I lay there, unconscious."

Jordan pressed a kiss to his lips. "I guess we'll have to ask her."

"Can you come by my house today?"

Thinking about her schedule, she nodded. "It'll be later, though. First I have to pick up two dogs from the groomer and deliver them to their owner, and then go feed a client's birds."

"I have an idea," Harry said. "Let me cook dinner for you tonight. I have a few more hours' work to finish up at the Tuckers' today. How about six-thirty at my place?"

Sounded like a date to her. Despite the cool autumn temperature, just being close to Harry warmed her from the inside out. "Sure. Text me the address."

After Harry walked Jordan to her car and gave her a sweet goodbye kiss, she headed to the dog grooming shop on Black Cat Boulevard. By the time she returned to the Tuckers' house, Harry had already left.

She took advantage of the alone time to take a leisurely shower then spent a little longer than usual dressing and doing her hair. Before she left, she played with the kittens and gave all the cats fresh food and water. "You guys behave while I'm gone, okay?"

We will, Rosin told her.

Milo head-butted her calf. *Have fun.*

"Thanks," she said. "I'm just helping Harry with something." The cats didn't need to know the specifics, or that he was making her dinner.

Fifteen minutes later, Jordan parked in front of Harry's cottage and took a few moments to absorb the mountain view. If she had to describe her dream home, this would be it. From the white split-rail fence surrounding the well-manicured yard to the twin window boxes spilling over with colorful snapdragons and pansies, everywhere she looked, she saw Harry's careful attention to detail.

Before she'd made it to the door, he opened it and gave her a warm smile. "Welcome." Stepping aside to let her pass, he said, "Thanks for coming."

Jordan inhaled his masculine scent as she entered the small entrance hall. Straight ahead was a mostly white kitchen. The island in the center of the room was set for two, with navy-colored plates and matching cloth napkins. "I love your house."

As Harry took her jacket, a white cat poked its head out from behind a wall. The feline studied her for several moments before approaching.

Jordan crouched down to let the cat smell her hand. "You must be Kitty." She smoothed the animal's silky coat. "Let's talk later, okay?"

Okay. Kitty walked away, stopping for a drink at her water bowl before leaving the room.

"She's shy with new people," Harry explained.

"That's fine. She'll talk to me." Jordan stood and took a better look at Harry. Wearing jeans and a royal blue polo shirt, he looked even more handsome than he had earlier.

"Can I get you some wine?"

"Yeah, whatever you have. Thanks." Jordan climbed onto one of the two barstools at the island, which she noticed was the only place to eat in the room, and she didn't see a dining room. "I'll assume that you don't entertain much."

Harry laughed as he uncorked a bottle of red wine. "That's an understatement. You might be my first dinner guest in three and a half years of renting this place." He poured the first glass and handed it to her.

Jordan waited until Harry had served himself before offering up a toast. "Cheers."

He tapped his glass to hers. "To discovering my past." Holding her stare, he drank.

Jordan wondered if once he learned where he'd come from — and who he was — if maybe the two of them could have a future. The wine was good — not too dry and not too sweet. She took in the décor, which was simple, clean, and unfussy. Thinking about her parents' kitchen, and Mallory's, she realized what was missing from Harry's. There were no family photos on the walls or the door of the fridge. Because he had no loved ones or at least none that he knew about. "How'd you come to live here, in this house?"

Harry's smile slipped a little. "I landed in Nocturne Falls purely by chance. I did odd jobs for a while, whatever I could get — helping at the loading dock at the DIY Depot, breaking down boxes for the Shop-n-Save, assorted repairs at a rundown motel." He scrubbed a hand over his face. "I did what I had to in order to survive."

Jordan touched his arm. "No judgment here."

"The owner of the Pinehurst Inn gave me a room in exchange for my help there. After a few months, I managed to scrape together enough cash to rent a small apartment in town."

Jordan took another sip of wine. "How'd you get from that to your own home and business?" Although she'd only lived in Nocturne Falls a year or so, she still hadn't managed to achieve a smidgeon of the success Harry had. Maybe she should be taking notes.

"Carpentry seemed to come naturally to me. Word of mouth did wonders, and it didn't take long for me to build a client base. I decided to take the exam to become a contractor." He went to the stove and lifted the lid off a pan. Delicious-smelling steam filled the air. "I have my own business, but this house is a rental."

"I'm still impressed." He didn't need to know that she was referring to more than his accomplishments. The man's rear view was just as hot as the front. She cleared her throat. "What's for dinner?"

"Nothing fancy," he said over his shoulder. "If I'd had more time, I'd have wowed you with my chicken cordon bleu. Maybe next time."

She liked the notion of them doing this again. "That would definitely wow me."

"Tonight we have kielbasa with peppers and potatoes."

"Yum." She mentally smacked her head. Why hadn't she thought to bring a bottle of wine or a dessert? Her mother had raised her better. "Next time I'll cook for you." She thought about her last kitchen debacle. "Or perhaps I'll order in."

Harry chuckled as he plated their dinner. "That sounds safer."

"Yeah," she agreed. "Probably true."

Kitty returned to the kitchen and rubbed against Harry's leg as he joined Jordan at the island.

At least Jordan would contribute something to the evening — whatever information the cat might have about Harry's identity. She bent down to pet the cat. "After dinner, you and I can get to know each other better, Miss Kitty."

The feline warily eyed Jordan then backed behind Harry. *No,* she said.

Uh oh. "Why not?" she asked the cat.

I don't like you.

Jordan scratched her head. She'd never encountered an animal that had taken an immediate dislike to her. After everything Harry had done for Jordan in the past couple of days, she didn't want to let him down. She met Harry's stare. "I'm not sure I can do this."

CHAPTER SEVEN

Harry's heart sank. "What's the problem?"

Jordan frowned. "She doesn't trust me."

"She's not used to being around anyone besides me."

"Not anyone?"

He was no saint. Sure, he'd briefly drowned his loneliness with the brunette who worked at the hat store in town, and he'd gone on a date with one of the waitresses from Salvatore's Pizza, only because she'd refused to take no for an answer. But admitting to Jordan that he could count on one hand the number of guests he'd entertained was a little embarrassing. "One or two."

"Hmm." Her expression was unreadable as she forked a bite of potatoes and sausage.

"Maybe I can reassure her that you're not a threat to her," he suggested.

Jordan shrugged. "That might work. I wouldn't blame her for being jealous."

He couldn't hold back a grin at Jordan's compliment. Setting down his napkin, he pushed away from the island then picked up the cat and cradled her against his chest. "You know that I love you, Kitty. Be a good girl, and I'll open a brand new catnip mouse for you."

The cat touched her paw to his chin.

Jordan's face lit up with a smile. "I think that did it."

"Great."

Kitty wriggled in his arms, so he let her down. He washed his hands before returning to his meal.

"This is delicious, by the way." Jordan ate the last of her food.

"Thanks." He liked that she had a healthy appetite and that she wasn't afraid to go for it. "You want more?"

"I'm saving room for dessert." She gestured toward the plate of chocolate chip cookies on the counter. "Did you bake those?"

"My neighbor dropped them off earlier."

Jordan raised an eyebrow. "Oh?"

Were there two jealous females in the room now? "It's not what you're thinking," he assured her. "She's a very kind middle-aged woman who works at home and has lots of time on her hands."

"Was that your attempt to reassure me?" Jordan folded her arms over her chest.

He was only getting himself in deeper. Clearing away their dishes, he asked if she wanted a refill on her wine.

"No thanks." Jordan joined him at the sink. "May I help?"

How could he think with her standing so close? He breathed in her sweet scent. "The dishes can wait." He twirled one of her blond curls around his finger and felt her shiver. As much as he itched to touch more of her, he had to put on the brakes, at least until he was sure that he wasn't someone Jordan should steer clear of. So he reached for the plate of cookies and offered it to her.

Jordan's shoulders sank as she helped herself to two. "Thanks." She set one on a napkin and bit into the other. "OMG." Closing her eyes, she moaned.

Harry couldn't help but hope that someday he'd elicit a similar reaction from her for a completely different reason. For now, he took solace in the chocolate chip nirvana.

Jordan polished off a third cookie then brushed off her hands. "I'm ready to begin the interrogation whenever you are."

Harry laughed. "I guess that's what it is." He showed Jordan into the living room where Kitty was curled up on the small rug in front of the fireplace. "Make yourself at home," he told Jordan.

"This is nice, cozy." She hugged her arms around her body as she sat on the sofa.

"Are you cold?" he asked.

"A little, but it's fine."

Since he kept the fireplace set up for a fire, all he had to do was light it. That done, he joined Jordan on the couch. "How do you do this?"

She patted his leg. "I just start a conversation with her."

His pulse kicked up a few notches, but he couldn't be sure if the cause were the anticipation of what they'd learn, or merely sitting so close to the sexy blond.

"Do you like the fire, Kitty?" Jordan asked.

The cat lifted her head and looked at Harry.

"Me, too," Jordan said. "Harry tells me that you were there with him when he woke up in the woods a few years ago. ... Mm-hmm...I see."

The moment felt surreal. Jordan was actually having a conversation with his cat. Harry had to know what Kitty had said. "What?"

"Kitty says that she was worried about you," Jordan told him. "She waited a long time for you to wake up."

Harry's heart pounded. "Did she see anyone there with me?"

Jordan looked at the cat and after a minute, nodded. "Oh," she said to Kitty. "I didn't realize that."

"She knows something?" he asked Jordan.

Jordan met Harry's stare. "Kitty says that another man—one with white hair—pointed a gun at you. You were asking the man why he was doing that, and how could he. He walked you to the edge of a cliff."

"And?" he asked.

Jordan flattened her lips. "The cat was sure that the man was going to hurt you, so she clawed his ankle. When he kicked her away, you ran."

Harry tried to recall something — anything — of the cat's story, but he didn't.

"Then what?" Jordan asked Kitty.

Harry dug his fingers into the sofa cushion as Jordan appeared to listen to whatever the cat was thinking...or saying. He didn't quite understand how it all worked.

Finally, Jordan thanked the cat then faced Harry. "You fell down a ravine. The man looked over the edge, but when Kitty heard another car coming, the man with the gun ran back to his van and sped away."

"When I came to, I was near the bottom of a cliff," Harry said. The cat had revealed just enough to pique his curiosity. "What about Kitty? Did she just happen upon the other man and me?"

"Is that when you first saw Harry?" Jordan asked the cat. She nodded slowly. "Oh, I didn't realize that."

Kitty jumped onto the coffee table and sat back on her haunches.

Jordan squeezed Harry's hand. "She was with you in the van. Your wrists had been bound together with rope or something, and there was tape covering your mouth. It was a long ride, and you'd managed to get your hands free and rip off the tape before the man opened the back. But he'd trained a gun on you, so you got out when he ordered you to."

"My wrists were bruised when I woke up. That explains how that happened."

Jordan leaned a little toward the cat. "Tell me about the van," she said. "Who was driving, and how'd you end up being a passenger?"

Harry looked from Jordan to his cat, and back again. Kitty wasn't even looking in Jordan's direction, but Jordan appeared to be responding to an unheard conversation. She alternately nodded, narrowed her eyes, and at one point, held her fist against her mouth.

Finally, she met Harry's gaze. "Good news and bad news."

"Give me the bad news first," he said.

"All right." She folded her hands on her lap. "Kitty said the driver was a tall, thin man. She didn't know him or you before that ride. The van was parked in an alley when Kitty saw a small lizard on the inside of the windshield. She found an open window and slipped inside. The man threw you into the back, and she thinks you were unconscious then."

He tried to process everything Jordan told him. If only he could remember something — anything — from that day. "What's the good news?"

A hopeful smile lifted the corners of Jordan's mouth. "She knows that the van had stripes on the outside, and where it was parked, or at least the general area."

He swallowed. "Yeah?"

Jordan nodded. "Up until that day, Kitty had spent all of her life in Florida."

"Florida," he echoed.

"Someplace called Cat's Paw Cove. Does that ring a bell?"

He rolled the name around in his head. "I wish it did, but no."

"It's okay because now we've got a jumping off point."

She was right. Drawing her into his arms, he held her tightly. "Thank you, Jordan. You're amazing. You've given me hope that I can find out who I am."

Backing out of his embrace, she looked up into his eyes. "That knowledge could change…" She dropped his gaze and caught her bottom lip between her teeth.

"What?"

"There's a chance that your past could impact us."

"I hope that it doesn't change anything between us, but you're right." He lifted her chin, so she had to look at him. "I probably should have made more of an effort to figure out who I am—or who I was. I suspect that I haven't until now because I'd grown too comfortable in my current situation. It was safer to bury my head in the sand and hope that I didn't used to be a bad person. Until now, the identity of my former self didn't matter all that much. You've given me a reason to want to move ahead with my life. And in order to do that, I have to be sure I wasn't someone who's not worthy of you."

Her eyes glistened. "In my heart, I'm sure that you could never have been anything but a good man, just as you are now."

He prayed that she was correct about that.

Jordan dried the pan Harry had just washed while he finished loading their dinner plates into the dishwasher. They had such an easy rapport as if they'd known each other for years, rather than only days. She liked Harry so much, but her past experience had shown her that she was usually a terrible judge of character. Every guy she'd dated had turned out to be wronger than wrong for her.

Heck, her poor decisions weren't limited to her love life. She did a fantastic job at sabotaging every job she'd worked and had even landed herself in legal trouble after acting upon her conscience and freeing a bunch of neglected animals from a zoo. Sure, helping them was the right thing to do. Too bad she hadn't thought of a better strategy, like organizing a boycott or a protest.

She'd also made so many mistakes in the way she'd treated her twin. Mallory had saved Jordan's life last year. The one silver lining of being kidnapped was that Jordan had come out of the situation with a new perspective on her relationship with her twin. Jordan loved Mal with all her heart. But despite her sisterly love, Jordan still managed to screw things up on a regular basis, like trying to cook breakfast and instead, burning down Mallory's kitchen.

Harry grasped her shoulders from behind and gently kissed the back of her neck.

His masculine scent and the feel of his whiskers on her skin conspired to turn on her inner pilot light.

"I can tell that you're worried," he said. "I promise you that I'll get to the bottom of this, and we'll roll with whatever punches are thrown at us."

She set down the pan and twisted around to return his kiss. He knew as well as she did that whatever he learned might very well slam the door on their budding romance. But she refused to discourage him from finding out who he was.

He held her at arms' length. "Are you up for some research on Cat's Paw Cove tonight?"

Harry didn't seem like the type of guy who spent a lot of time on computers. The least she could do was to help him. Plus, she was curious. "Of course."

His face brightened with a smile. "I'll be right back."

Kitty strode into the room and sniffed at her food bowl, which still had a few nuggets of kibble in it. *I want food.*

Jordan chuckled to herself. "Cats and people have a different concept of what empty means. Why don't you eat what's in your dish?"

The cat sat down. *I want more.*

"I'll pass along the request to Harry." She hung the damp dishtowel over the oven door handle. "So what's Cat's Paw Cove like?"

Lots of fishermen, Kitty replied. *And good scraps.*

"Is it on the ocean or the gulf?"

I don't know.

Of course, she didn't. Most cats and dogs didn't understand things like that. "Sorry."

When Harry returned to the kitchen, he had a laptop tucked under one arm, and a plastic zipper bag with a paper inside in the other hand.

Kitty weaved in front of him, trying to steer him to her bowl.

"I already fed you tonight," Harry told the cat, which didn't deter Kitty from her mission at all. He set the computer on the island and handed Jordan the bag. "When I woke up, this note was the only thing in my pocket. Unfortunately, it was a rainy night, and all I managed to see before the ink washed away was the name, Harry. Or rather, most of the name. It actually said H-a-r-r."

While Harry booted up the laptop, Jordan gingerly removed the yellowed paper from the bag and examined it. Only a few dark smudges remained of whatever had been written, but unlike modern paper, Harry's felt more like cloth. She carefully returned it to the bag. "Not much to go on. I'd lay odds that your letter is pretty old, though."

Harry exhaled loudly. "That's what I think. Before the 1850s, most paper was made from recycled linen and cotton rags."

"Sounds like you've done research on the subject."

"A little. Since the paper is a lot older than I am, I can't imagine why I'd have been carrying it around. Now I'm curious about that town."

"Cat's Paw Cove." She gestured at the laptop. "May I?"

"Be my guest." He moved the computer closer to her.

She Googled the name of the town. The page populated with links. She clicked on a photo of a charming street lined with shops that reminded Jordan of Nocturne Falls, but without the Halloween motifs. There was a beauty salon similar to the Hair Scare, where Mallory worked, and a restaurant with a sidewalk patio area. "Seems like a nice place," she said.

Harry remained silent for a few moments. "Looks can be deceiving."

Had he remembered something from his past? "What do you mean?"

Lines fanned out from the corners of his eyes. "If I was kidnapped in Cat's Paw Cove, how nice a town could it be? And if that's where I'm from—or at least where I'd been living—why haven't any of my friends or family there been searching for me?"

She covered his hand with hers. "You can't be sure of that. Perhaps they have been looking for you."

Tiny muscles around his jaw ticked. "For years I've regularly checked the online missing person message boards. My picture isn't on any of them."

The pain in his expression cut straight through her. She wished there was something she could do to help. Glancing down at the plastic bag with the blank paper inside, she got an idea. "I know a couple of psychics. How would you feel if we showed your letter to them? Maybe they'll pick up on something."

A spark of hope brightened his expression. "Why not? When can we do that?"

She checked the time on the computer. It was past nine-thirty, too close to her early-bird twin's bedtime. "First thing in the morning. My sister works at the Hair Scare salon. She reads tarot cards, and her friend Darcy is a palm reader. One of the hairdressers does scrying."

"How did I get so lucky to have a gorgeous woman with so many great ideas just fall out of the sky into my arms?" Harry pulled her into a hug then pressed his lips to hers.

She felt like the lucky one. "Right time, right place."

Harry gave her another kiss—one that tempted her to stay there with him all night. Before they got too carried away, she centered a hand on his chest to ease him back. Too bad that touching his rock-hard pecs only made it more difficult.

But she had responsibilities. Plus, this time she refused to take things too fast. "I should get back to the Tuckers' place."

Harry frowned. "We can't be sure it's safe. Until the police catch the man who broke in last night, I don't think you ought to be alone there."

He had a point.

"Give me five minutes," he said. "I'll pack a bag and go with you." Without waiting for her to object, he left the room.

Having Harry spend another night on the sofa was going to test her resolve, but he was right. The notion of being in that big house all by herself didn't thrill her. She drew a deep breath. This was going to be tough.

CHAPTER EIGHT

Harry tossed and turned most of the night on the Tuckers' sofa. How was he supposed to sleep with so many unanswered questions tumbling around in his head? He'd never even considered consulting a psychic about his past, probably because he hadn't believed in such things — until he'd met a genuine cat whisperer.

Jordan. She was another reason he couldn't shut off his mind — or his libido. Did she have any idea what an incredible gift she'd given him by opening the first door to his past?

During the night, she'd come downstairs for a glass of water, and they'd ended up lip-locked for several minutes. He'd managed to muster all of his resolve not to take it further. Just thinking about it — about her — was getting him hot and bothered all over again. He needed a cold shower, or at least, a dip in the pool. All he could do was pray that once he discovered his former identity, he'd learn that he'd been the kind of guy Jordan deserved, and not someone dangerous or smarmy.

On his way to the bathroom, he stopped at the front window to take in the view. Sunrise painted the horizon in ribbons of pink, orange, and gold. He was about to walk away when he noticed a dark sedan parked on the street. Goosebumps spread over his arms. The car looked a lot like the one that had been following him the day before, but with dark, tinted windows, he still couldn't make out the driver.

He ran back to the study to retrieve his phone. Grabbing the poker from the fireplace, he went back to the window.

The car was gone. Which convinced him even more that it had been the person who'd followed him, and had broken into the house. Harry clenched his jaw. Without knowing if the man was after him or Jordan, he didn't dare leave her alone for a minute. If he planned to shadow her when she went to walk her clients' dogs or feed their cats, he'd have to get an early start on his own work here.

After a quick shower, he dressed in his work clothes then retrieved his tools from the truck. He managed to finish sanding down the built-in bookcases before Jordan came downstairs.

"Morning," she murmured in a sleep-soaked voice. Even with disheveled hair, and dark make-up smudges under her eyes, she stole his breath.

He cleared the cobwebs from his throat. "Good morning. Did you sleep well?"

Her cheeks grew rosy, and she diverted her gaze. "Um, yeah."

"There's coffee."

Without a word, she shuffled toward the kitchen, her bunny slippers rasping on the wooden floorboards.

He heard her pour herself a cup.

"I texted my sister," she called to him. "She can squeeze you in for a quickie reading at nine."

He checked his watch. That gave them a little more than an hour before they had to be there. "You'll come with me, won't you?"

She appeared in the doorway holding a large coffee mug with both hands. "I figured you'd want some privacy. I thought I'd take care of my clients while you were at the Hair Scare."

Although he didn't want to frighten her, she had a right to know that someone was watching one of them. Even though Harry was probably the man's target, that didn't mean Jordan was safe. "I need to tell you something."

After he'd shared his suspicions about the car that had been out front earlier, Jordan squared her shoulders. "You're right. I'll go to your reading."

A little of the tension in his shoulders relaxed. "And I can join you on your rounds to see your clients."

An hour later, he pulled open the door to the Hair Scare and waited for Jordan to go through. The strong smell of hairspray filled the air. The place was busy. Every hair station was occupied, and the noise level was high, with the din of blow dryers and people trying to talk over them. Two women and a man sat in the waiting area, but the two nail stations on the far side of the business weren't being used at the moment.

"Hey!" Mallory strode toward them. "Nice to see you again, Harry." She gave Jordan a hug.

"Thanks for doing this," Jordan said to her twin.

"No worries, but unfortunately, I don't have time for a full reading. We'll do what we can, though." To Harry, she said, "Come on over to my table."

Taking Jordan's hand, he followed her sister.

"Sure you want me to hear this?" Jordan asked him.

"I am." He pulled another chair over to the table so they could both sit opposite Mallory.

Mallory handed him a large deck of cards. "Shuffle them as you think about what it is you want to know. When you're finished, cut the deck twice."

He concentrated on specific questions as he mixed the cards: Who was I before the amnesia? Why was I kidnapped? Then he set them down on the table and made three stacks. "Okay."

Mallory took one pile and turned over several cards, staring at them for a minute or so. "It's your past you're interested in, right?"

"Yes."

"This is very interesting." She tapped one of the cards that showed a nervous-looking cat sitting on a scale in an exam room. "The five of Swords is all about mind games and hostility. And the three of Swords represents betrayal."

The second card she touched depicted a hungry-looking cat approaching a boarded-up cottage. His gaze slid over to the next card, The Tower, where a cat plummeted toward the ground. "That doesn't look good."

Mallory frowned. "Well, it's not, particularly with these others."

When he noticed that the next card was labeled Death, he gulped.

Mallory pointed to it. "That doesn't mean what you think. The Death card indicates change, the end of something."

"Or someone?" What if he'd killed a person? His gut clenched.

"No, I don't think you killed somebody." She glanced toward the door and nodded at someone. "My client is here, so we'll have to wrap this up soon."

"Of course," he told Mallory.

Mallory stared at the cards for another moment before looking at Harry and Jordan. "What I can tell you about your past is that you had a person or persons in your life who coveted what you had. You weren't aware of their jealousy, and because you had no idea, they were able to set in motion a series of events that crashed your world down around you."

Jordan squeezed his hand.

Mallory gathered the cards. "If you want to come back tomorrow, I'll have more time and we can look at your present and future."

His head pounded. "I-I'll call you." He tried paying Mallory, but she refused any money for the reading.

After they left, Jordan suggested they stop at The Hallowed Bean for coffee and a bite to eat.

"Yeah, sure," he said. Maybe a shot of caffeine would help him think straight and come up with a plan of attack. They went inside and got in line behind a woman with blue hair and pointy prosthetic ears. At least, he hoped they were prosthetic. Sure looked real from behind.

When it was their turn, Jordan ordered a Dracu-latté and a Franken-Frosted cookie.

"I'll have the same," Harry told the barista as he took out his wallet.

Jordan shook her head at him. "This is my treat. You bought my entire family lunch yesterday, remember?"

When he started to protest, she set her hands on her hips and frowned.

"Okay, fine," he said. "You win." They carried their order to a table. He held her chair out for her.

Jordan sat down and whistled. "What a gentleman. Thank you."

She ought to be used to men treating her with courtesy and respect, but he suspected that she wasn't. His gut tightened a little. He took a bite of the cookie, which melted in his mouth.

"What'd you think of the reading?" Jordan asked.

"That what your sister said makes sense. If there was someone in Cat's Paw Cove who was jealous of whatever I had, maybe he took it upon himself to try to kill me."

Jordan licked a crumb from her upper lip, reminding him how incredibly kissable that gorgeous mouth was. "I did more research on Cat's Paw Cove last night after I went upstairs. They've got a local newspaper called the *Cat's Paw Cove Carrier*. It's available online as well as in print. I went back four and a half years, but there was nothing about any locals turning up missing."

He wrapped his hands around his drink. "Maybe I wasn't from there."

Jordan slowly nodded. "That could be it." She popped the last bite of her cookie into her mouth.

"Since I have no idea what my name used to be, I wouldn't know where to being searching."

"It's a small town," she said. "Perhaps if we go there we'll be able to find more clues."

We? "I don't want to pull you into something that might be dangerous."

She narrowed those blue eyes at him and scowled. "First of all, you're not forcing me to do something I don't want to. Secondly, I'm not some weak, can't-take-care-of-herself waif."

"Should I remind you how we met? You were literally about to fall, possibly to your death." Okay, that was an exaggeration, but he'd made his point.

Jordan squared her shoulders. "You're going to need me there, or at least, my gift."

"Am I?"

She scraped together the crumbs from her cookie and ate them. "Absolutely. Animals see and hear things that we don't. Your own cat is the perfect example. All these years you had no idea that your own pet held clues to what happened to you."

She had a point. And in truth, he couldn't leave her alone at the Tuckers' house. Which reminded him what she was doing at said house. "What about the Tuckers' cats? Cat's Paw Cove is over four hundred miles away. We might not be able to make the round trip in one day, especially if we need to spend more than a couple of hours there."

"I can message Mrs. Tucker to make sure it's okay with her, as long as we'll be back in a day or so. I'm pretty sure Mallory or my friend Darcy would be willing to go by the house a couple times a day and take care of the cats."

Having Jordan with him would set his mind at ease that she was safe. Harry gathered their trash and threw it away. By the time he returned to the table, Jordan was sending a message from her phone.

Wearing a smug grin, she stood. "As soon as I hear back from everyone, we can plan our little trip."

"The one I haven't yet agreed to?" He pulled open the door and ushered her through.

"That's the one." She strode a few feet ahead of him on Black Cat Boulevard then stopped and took out her phone. "Mrs. Tucker is fine with me going away for a day or two as long as I can get her kitties covered."

Using his key fob, he unlocked his truck and opened the passenger side door for

Jordan. He offered her a hand up, which she took.

Her phone chirped with a message. As soon as she sat in the cab, she took out her cell and smiled down at it. "We're good. Mallory and her fiance would be happy to pick up my cat-sitting duties, and even help out with my other clients while we're away. We can leave today, as long as that's all right with you."

"You mean I have a choice in all of this?" He resisted a chuckle.

A playful grin lifted one side of her sexy lips. "Of course you do, silly." She pulled her door shut.

As he circled the truck and climbed inside, his whole body tingled with anticipation. Tomorrow might very well be the day he found out who he was. He just prayed that he'd finally be able to look forward to a future without worrying about his past.

Jordan checked the navigation app on her phone again. They'd left Nocturne Falls a few minutes after one in the afternoon, and so far they were making good time, even though Harry was driving her car slower than she would. She'd suggested he take the first shift, mostly because he seemed antsy, and she'd figured that driving would be better for him than merely staring out the car windows. Four hours into their trip, he seemed perfectly content to stay at the wheel.

She glanced into the back seat where Kitty had curled up and gone to sleep a little while after they'd gotten on the road. "Your cat is a champion passenger. Mallory's cat, Hazel, would be hanging by her claws from the headliner by now."

"Kitty's used to riding with me. During our first month or two in Nocturne Falls, she went everywhere with me. I think she was afraid to let me out of her sight." He passed a slow-moving truck. "What time does your app say we should reach our destination?"

"About eight o'clock if the weather and traffic conditions hold up."

Kitty popped her head up a moment before a bolt of lightning lit up the horizon. Massive grey storm clouds came out of nowhere. The traffic slowed to a crawl as the heavens opened up and a monsoon moved in.

"I guess I should have kept my mouth shut," Jordan quipped.

They crossed into Florida at a snail's pace. Four hours later, the rain finally let up.

"Look!" Jordan pointed to the sign announcing the town. "Welcome to Cat's Paw Cove, established 1625."

"Hmph." Harry slowed their speed.

"What is it?" she asked him.

"I was hoping for…I don't know, a spark of familiarity." His brow knitted. "Something."

Jordan patted his thigh. "Maybe when you see more of it. Give it time."

They drove along Whiskers Lane, past a bookstore called Tales, and other businesses with feline-themed names, like Cat's Eye Jewelry Shop, and Claws-N-Coifs Salon. Loads of delicious-looking confections filled the display window of a closed bakery tempted Jordan. "This place is adorable," she said. With a glance back at the bakery, she set her hand over her suddenly-growling belly.

Harry turned left onto Sherwood Boulevard, where there were even more quaint shops.

"It certainly appears to be charming." Harry gestured toward a lighted sign on a high stone wall announcing Sherwood Manor. "I wonder what that is."

In the dark, Jordan couldn't make out more than a lush garden path beyond the imposing wrought iron gates. "Whatever it is, it looks fancy." She rolled down her window and breathed in the beach-scented breeze. Kitty jumped onto her lap and purred. Jordan petted the cat's back.

A small crowd milled around the sidewalk in front of a restaurant up ahead. The aromas of burgers and tummy fried foods reminded Jordan that she hadn't eaten anything besides a cookie in the morning, and then a pack of cheese and crackers from a convenience store along the highway. "I'm starving." She read the neon sign with the flashing cat on it. "Purry's Burgers. I'm game."

"Why not." Harry parked on the street then opened a backpack-style cat carrier, and Kitty hopped into it. Her adorable face filled the clear plastic bubble near the top.

"That looks like fun," Jordan said to the cat.

It's okay, Kitty told her. *At least I can go places in it where people don't usually let cats. People can be snobs!*

"I'd let you go anywhere it's safe," Jordan told the cat.

"What?" Harry asked.

Jordan shook her head. "Nothing. Kitty likes the backpack."

Inside, *Earth Angel* played on the old-fashioned jukebox. A rotating glass display case on the long counter showcased gigantic slices of coconut cake, lemon meringue pie, and huge chocolate brownies.

A dark-haired waitress wearing an iconic red and white checkered uniform with a white apron approached them holding a couple of menus. She narrowed her eyes at the cat carrier then just smiled. "Counter or booth?"

Harry took Jordan's hand. "Booth, please."

The middle-aged woman's shoes squeaked on the black and white tile floor as she led them to a booth upholstered with sparkly red vinyl. "We've got the Sherwood Burger on special tonight, and buy one, get one free tuxedo milkshakes." She set down the menus on the table as Harry set the backpack on the seat before sliding into the booth.

"Tuxedo milkshake?" Jordan asked.

"Black and white," she replied. "Chocolate and vanilla. And we make 'em the old fashioned way, a million times better than those ready-made ones that come straight out of a machine. I'll give y'all a minute. My name's Charlene." She melted into a passing group of high school-aged boys all dressed in light blue football uniforms.

"I love this place!" Jordan flipped open her menu. "It's like we've stepped back in time."

When Harry winced, she realized her comment had probably hit a nerve.

"Sorry," she said. "I didn't mean—"

He shook his head. "I know. It's fine. I just wish all of this felt familiar."

A lump lodged in her throat. She scanned the menu, and when Charlene returned, Jordan and Harry ordered the daily specials.

Their waitress brought the tuxedo milkshakes and a saucer of water for Kitty.

Harry thanked the woman. He unzipped the backpack and lifted Kitty out with her leash and harness on then set her on the seat so she could get to her drink.

Jordan slipped a straw into her milkshake, which was brown on one side and white on the other. "I wonder how they do that." She sucked in a taste and moaned with pleasure. "OMG. That's the best. Try it."

Harry took a sip, rolling his eyes heavenward as he did. "Sure is."

Charlene returned with two giant cheeseburgers complete with giant servings of fries and coleslaw.

They barely spoke as they devoured their dinner as if they hadn't eaten in days. Finally, Jordan gave up and pushed her plate to the edge of the table. "I really want the rest of those fries, but I think I'll explode if I have another one."

"They're too good to waste." Harry scooped up her leftovers.

Jordan wiped up the condensation her drink had left. "What's the plan now?"

He shrugged. "Since we've arrived later than I'd planned, and most of the town is closed for the night, we'll have to start in the morning. I think we should see what local records are available. We passed a town hall on Sherwood Boulevard."

Jordan swiped one last French fry and bit off the end. "Sound good. And maybe we can check out some of the shops." When he balked at that, she explained. "Perhaps someone will recognize you."

Laughing, he piled his empty plate on top of hers. "I'm sure that's your motive. That must explain your oohs and ahs when we passed by those stores, right?"

Her face heated. "Sure, that was it."

The waitress came to collect their dishes. "Did y'all save room for a slice of Purry's pecan pie or catnip coconut cake?"

Jordan sank lower in the seat. "I wish."

As soon as she set down their bill, Harry grabbed it. "Can you recommend a motel around here?"

Her lips bunched to one side. "Your best bet is the Catnap Motel. It's clean and reasonable, but most places are gonna be booked up this weekend."

"Why?" Jordan asked.

Charlene looked at her as if Jordan had a spider in the middle of her forehead.

"Tomorrow's the hundredth anniversary of Coquina Castle."

"I read about that place," Harry said. "An eccentric millionaire built it for his bride, but she left him only days after their wedding. To this day, no one knows how he created the rock gardens all by himself."

Charlene nodded her agreement. "It's a magical place. They just finished a big restoration, too, which is why so many people are in town for the anniversary celebration."

Harry handed the waitress cash then loaded his cat into the carrier. "We'd better get over there soon then."

"Good luck," Charlene said. "Take a left on Sherwood. The motel will be on the left just before A1A, right across the road from Surf's Up Café."

After they left Purry's, Harry took Kitty out of her carrier and attached a leash to her harness. "I'm sure we can find a sandy patch over there." He gestured toward a small park across the street.

"Mind if I check out the shopping landscape?" Jordan asked. "It's much safer for me to do that while the stores are closed."

Harry chuckled then reeled her in for a quick kiss. "I'll meet you back at the car in fifteen minutes. Be aware of your surroundings."

She saluted him. "Yes, sir!"

"I'm serious."

"I know. And I promise I'll be careful." Heading away from Purry's, Jordan stopped to ogle the baubles in the display window of Cat's Eye Jewelry. She continued on, passing an antique shop and a beachy clothing store. Peering around a corner, she noticed a small courtyard with a fountain and wrought iron tables and chairs. A bent cat's paw dangling from the streetlamp post pointed into the alley. A ship-shaped sign marked the charming section as Calico Court.

Jordan glanced around. Plenty of people strolled the streets. She felt perfectly safe to check out the charming alcove. Pots spilled over with colorful flowers, and several strings of fairy lights strung in a star shape overhead gave the place a warm, welcoming feel. One doorway opened into an upscale restaurant called Medici, but the three other businesses were closed—The Zen Den yoga and meditation studio, Eye of Newt, which appeared to be a metaphysical store, and the Cove Cat Café.

Sitting on the edge of the fountain, she took in the soothing sound of the water, and the sweet scent of the Confederate jasmine vines.

I could totally live here.

Movement in the window of the café caught her eye. Was that a cat? It was. There were at least half a dozen felines inside.

131

Jordan went closer to investigate and cupped her hands over the glass to see inside. The café was split into two parts—one was a room with every imaginable type of cat furniture and toy. The other half of the business appeared to be a small coffee house.

She crouched by the window to speak to the cats that had gathered on the other side of the glass. "What is this place?"

People come here to adopt us, a Scottish fold told her.

And to play with us, a white kitten said.

"That's the coolest thing ever!"

A torbie—a mix of tortoiseshell and tabby—put his front paws against the glass. *We like it.*

The loud chime of a clock reminded her that it was time to return to the car to meet Harry. "I have to go now," she told the cats, feeling a little like Cinderella leaving the ball. Except she was heading to meet her Prince Charming, not running *from* him "But I'll come back tomorrow to visit." When she got to her car, Harry was just opening the back door for Kitty.

He smiled at Jordan, giving her that champagne bubble feeling in her belly. "Hey," he said. "Find anything interesting?" He handed her the car keys.

She sat behind the wheel as Harry slid into the passenger seat. "Lots of awesome stores." But this wasn't a vacation. They were on the hunt for information. She'd tell him all about the cat café later. "I'll check online and find out what time the town hall opens tomorrow."

"Good, thanks."

Jordan drove straight to the Catnap Motel, which reminded her of any other roadside motel, except for the sign in the shape of a curled-up cat.

Inside the small, seventies-era lobby, a grey-haired man sitting behind the counter looked over his wire-rimmed glasses at them. "Evening, folks."

Harry approached him. "Good evening. We'd like two rooms, please."

The clerk frowned. "I'm full up, just like every other hotel and bed and breakfast in the area."

Jordan exchanged a worried glance with Harry.

"Your best bet is St. Augustine," the man advised.

"That's at least an hour away, isn't it?" Jordan asked.

"Yup." The man typed on his keyboard. "Oh, wait. We just had a cancellation, but it's a single."

"We'll take it," Harry said.

Jordan froze. Sharing a room might be awkward. She wasn't ready to take their new relationship to the next level yet.

"Do you have a roll-away?" Harry handed the clerk his credit card.

"I'll bring it over," he said. "You'll be in sixteen, around the back."

After Jordan parked in front of the room, Harry brought Kitty inside and set up bowls of food and water for the cat. Jordan carried in her laptop and overnight bag, along with Harry's.

Her mouth grew dry as she sat on the bed. Sure, Harry had spent two nights at the Tuckers' house with her, but they'd been in separate rooms, on different floors. This was a whole new ballgame.

When the clerk knocked on the door, Harry opened it and relieved the man of the roll-away bed. "Good night."

Seeing how small and rickety the portable bed appeared, Jordan stood up. "I can sleep on that. It doesn't look big enough for you."

"I wouldn't dream of subjecting you to this." He wheeled it to the window then opened it up and started putting on the sheets.

She swallowed past the lump in her throat. "At least let me help." Making hospital corners at the foot of the cot, she noticed a wrinkle in the center of Harry's forehead, just above his nose. "Sure you're okay? I really don't mind taking the roll-away."

Again, he waved off her offer. "No, it isn't that." He folded his tall frame into the only chair in the room.

"What then?"

He rubbed the bridge of his nose. "If I used to live here, someone should recognize me. No one we've seen tonight has."

Jordan crouched down in front of him and patted his thigh. "We just got here, and only a few people have seen you tonight. Besides, more than eight thousand people live in this town. And this is Florida. A huge percentage of the population is transient in this state. Maybe the waitress at Purry's has only lived here a short time."

Smiling, he cupped her face in his hand. "You're right."

She pushed herself up and went to take out her laptop. "I've got a feeling that tomorrow will be the day. We can check out that festival the waitress told us about. I'd lay odds that lots of locals will be there, and if you used to live here, someone will recognize you."

CHAPTER NINE

Harry rolled onto his left side, and the cot springs squeaked loudly. There was no getting comfortable on the thin, lumpy mattress. And the threadbare curtains were useless against the fluorescent lamp outside the door. Didn't matter that he was exhausted. A few feet away, Jordan softly sighed. Maybe having her so close, but not being able to touch her was contributing to his sleeplessness. Or his disappointment that no one they'd met in Cat's Paw Cove had recognized him. If only he could turn off his mind for a little while.

He closed his eyes again and attempted to clear all thoughts and distractions. Seconds ticked past at a snail's pace. Until he conjured an image of Jordan—her silky blond locks, slender figure, and those captivating blue eyes. Drawing a deep breath, he caught a whiff of her coconut scent. In his mind's eye, he saw those plump, pink lips, and he couldn't resist kissing them.

Great, now he needed a cold shower. He punched his pillow and shifted onto his back.

"Harry?" Jordan whispered.

"Yeah?"

"You can't sleep, can you?" She sat up and switched on the bedside lamp.

He swiped a hand over his chin and yawned. "I guess I have too much on my mind. I hope all my tossing and turning didn't wake you."

Shaking her head, she gestured at the roll-away. "I had a feeling that you wouldn't be able to sleep on that thing. Come on." She patted the mattress.

Tempting as her offer was, he wouldn't risk her heart by taking the next step with her. If they made love and then discovered that he had a checkered past, he'd have to walk away. And Jordan wouldn't be the only one left with a broken heart.

What if Cat's Paw Cave was a dead end? Just because Kitty said that Harry was taken from the town didn't necessarily mean that was where he'd lived. His odyssey might not lead them to his past.

He liked Jordan so much. She deserved more than a big question mark.

He sat up. "You ought to be with a guy who takes you on real dates, not fact-finding missions."

"Oh, please." She rolled her eyes and grinned. "All I'm offering here is a comfier bed."

Despite his resolve to keep her at arms' length for the time being, he desperately needed sleep. Besides, exhausted as he was, he had no energy for anything else. "You're sure you don't mind?"

"I don't make this offer to many men." She threw him a wink. Come on."

He tamped down his reservations and peeled back the covers. "Thank you." As he slipped into bed next to her, he felt her warmth.

"Night," she murmured as she rolled onto her side.

"Good night." He shut his eyes, but his pulse was racing. So much for the more comfortable bed. As long as Jordan was next to him—close enough to touch, all he could think about was the feel of her silky hair and the taste of her tongue.

"Hold me," she whispered softly.

Had he imagined that? She appeared to be sleeping, her breaths coming in a steady cadence.

Harry propped himself on one elbow. "Jordan?"

She pushed aside the covers and faced him.

How could he have missed that white, lacy nightgown? He could have sworn she'd been wearing shorts and a tank top. "When did you?—"

Pressing a finger to his lips, she said, "Shh. Just kiss me."

Was he dreaming? Had to be. So he grasped her waist and eased her on top of him. Every nerve and fiber in his body hummed with desire. In the back of his mind, warning bells sounded, but he couldn't stop himself. For so long, he'd kept his carnal needs at bay. No other woman had tempted him, not like Jordan did.

She leaned down to kiss him, but instead of his mouth, she pressed her lips to his ear. "Sweet dreams."

What?

He smelled coffee.

"Rise and shine."

He'd only been dreaming. Relief and regret warred inside him as he peeled open his eyes.

Jordan sat on the edge of the mattress. Her hair was damp, and she smelled like fresh strawberries. Wearing jeans and a cornflower blue T-shirt the same shade as her eyes, she set a mug on the bedside table. "You talk in your sleep."

He pushed himself up and leaned against the headboard. "Should I be worried?"

"Should I? You spoke my name."

Stifling a chuckle, he grinned. "My dream was just getting to the good part when I woke up."

She lowered her gaze, and a pink flush rose in her cheeks. "The town hall is only open until noon on Saturdays, so we should probably get going soon."

"Of course." He drank a few sips of coffee then went to take a shower. Less than forty-five minutes later, they arrived at the Cat's Paw Cove town hall, only to find the place closed for a 'special event.'

Harry's mood clunked. "Dead end, at least until Monday."

Jordan hooked his arm. "We can look somewhere else for now. What about that celebration? Some castle."

"Right. I think we passed a poster about that." He spotted the announcement on a lamppost near the town hall. "There."

Jordan beat him to the spot. "In a small town like this, half the residents will probably be at this event. But..." Her lips bunched to one side.

He adjusted the backpack cat carrier. "But what?"

Jordan set her hands on her hips. "Perhaps you should disguise yourself."

"In case whoever tried to kill me happens to be there?"

"Well, yes. And there might be others at the celebration,"

"You're right. We passed a drugstore last night. I bet they'll have something I could use."

Jordan nodded. "Cheshire Apothecary. I think it's on Whiskers Lane."

At the store, they found what they needed—dark sunglasses and a baseball cap for him, and a wide-brimmed sun hat for Jordan. That done, they followed the signs to Coquina Castle.

On Sherwood Boulevard, Harry spotted a small sign pointing to a winding road. "This is it." He drove slowly, offering up a silent prayer that the place would spark a memory for him. Harry parked in an overflow lot.

Jordan gathered her long hair into a ponytail then put on her hat. "How's this?"

"You look like an adorable tourist." He gave her a kiss before attaching Kitty's leash to her harness and getting out.

Food stands and a few other vendors lined the grassy path that led to the entrance. Several small groups of people stood near the high stone wall, chatting, and taking pictures. Harry stepped up to a ticket booth manned by a middle-aged blonde. "Two, please," he told the woman.

"That'll be thirty-six dollars." The woman handed Jordan a brochure.

Harry paid their admission then they went under a large banner announcing the hundredth anniversary, toward the open gate.

Jordan gasped as they walked through into an open-air, fortress-like park. "Holy cow!"

"You took the words out of my mouth." Everywhere he looked, he found massive carved stone statues, chairs, fountains, and monoliths. The structures were arranged in separate areas, or vignettes, complete with topiaries, and formal gardens.

"Check this out." Jordan led him through a stone doorway with a giant coquina 'door' hinged at the middle of the bottom and top. She pushed on the left side of the slab, which had to weigh several tons. Miraculously, the stone turned as easily as a revolving door.

Jordan sat on a chair carved out of the rock and read the brochure. "No one knows how the man who built this place, Charles Lingor, managed to move all the stone from a quarry ten miles from here, or how he was able to create the mechanisms like the one that opens that monster of a door with hardly any effort."

"It's amazing." But Harry was more interested in the people milling around the site. A group of five young women—all wearing too much make-up and jewelry—strode past him, talking and laughing. Several families with young children took in the sights. A tall, middle-aged woman with jet-black hair narrowed her eyes at Harry, then blanched and ducked behind a moon-shaped topiary.

Harry's gut tightened. Had the woman recognized him? If she had, why wouldn't she have approached him? Nausea swirled inside him. He sat down next to Jordan until the feeling passed. He scanned the spot where the black-haired woman has been, but he didn't see her anymore.

"Are you okay?" Jordan asked him.

He shrugged. "Maybe I need to eat, or maybe drink."

"I'll go get you some water," she offered. She took the cat's leash from Harry.

"I'm okay." When he stood, a headache stabbed at his temples. "Let's check out the food vendors outside."

Harry found a picnic table near the gate while Jordan got him a calzone, an ice tea from the Pie in the Sky booth, a bowl of cool water for Kitty.

Jordan set his food down in front of him. "I'll be right back." She handed him Kitty's leash. "Please don't wait for me. Go ahead and dig in."

She didn't have to tell him twice. He was used to working in the Georgia heat, and he didn't always eat breakfast the moment he got out of bed in the morning, so he had no idea why his head was pounding.

Jordan returned with a bag from Sugarland Bakery. "I got two black and white cookies and one toffee toll house square."

He cut the calzone in half, and gooey, white cheese oozed from the scars. "Breakfast of champions, hmm?" He pulled

143

off a small piece of cheese and fed it to his cat before taking his own bite.

Jordan ate a piece and moaned. "OMG, this is so good."

After he'd eaten a few bites, his headache eased. "I saw someone in the gardens, a woman."

"Yeah? Someone you know?" Jordan broke off a big chunk of the calzone and popped the whole piece into her mouth.

"I'm not sure. She disappeared before I could speak to her." Rubbing the bridge of his nose, he tried to recall the woman's face: strong cheekbones, pointy nose, greenish-blue eyes.

Eyes that remind me of my own.

A chill rolled over his skin. He scanned the people milling about the area but didn't see the woman.

Jordan touched his arm. "Are you sure you're all right?"

Not really. "Yeah, fine."

"What do you want to do after this?"

Harry broke off a piece of the toll house square. "Let's take another look around."

Jordan folded her arms over her chest. "There's something you're not telling me."

She already knew him well. "The woman I noticed earlier..."

Jordan blanched. "Were you married to her?"

"No, nothing like that. Actually, she's a lot older than I. It was her eyes."

"Her eyes?"

Swallowing the sweet treat, he nodded. "They reminded me of mine."

Understanding registered in her expression. "Perhaps she's your mother. But if she is, wouldn't she have spoken to you?"

"I don't know." He ate the cookie in a few bites.

Jordan set her hand over her stomach. "I'm so full." She slipped what was left of the sweets back into the bag while Harry gathered their trash and threw it into the nearby can. "Let's go back in," Jordan said.

But after a half-hour search of the property, they didn't find the woman. Jordan sat on a stone bench. "What now?"

"Wasn't there something online about a local museum or history center?"

"Mm-hmm." Jordan took out her phone and started typing on it. "The Shipwreck Museum is scheduled to open next year on A1A," she read. "Until then, visitors can learn about the history of Cat's Paw Cove at a temporary exhibit at Wilshire Park."

"Let's go," Harry said.

As they strode toward the parking area, he noticed a tall brunette getting into a blue SUV. He wished she'd turn around so he could see her face. "That might be her."

The woman glanced at them over her shoulder then yanked her car door closed and took off.

"Let's go." Harry picked up the cat, and he and Jordan ran the rest of the way to Jordan's car. "I'd like to drive."

She got in the passenger side and handed the keys to Harry. Driving as fast as he dared on the dirt road, he clenched his jaw. The SUV was gone.

When they reached the main road, Harry pounded his fists on the steering wheel. "Damn it."

Jordan patted his thigh. "She could have only turned right or left. Pick one."

He took a left. After driving several miles, he gave up. His shoulders sank. "The fact that she hauled ass out of there confirms that she knows me."

"I agree," Jordan muttered. "She looked…spooked when she did."

Jordan was right. He wondered if she'd been afraid of him—or if he should be afraid of her.

"I guess we should check out the exhibit at Wilshire Park." He made a U-turn and drove toward Whiskers Lane. When they arrived at the park, he noticed what he hadn't the night before—a tall brick tower with an old-fashioned sailing ship at the top that was actually a clock. "Can't be much of an exhibit."

Jordan nodded her agreement. "It looks pretty small." She twisted around to look at Kitty. "Really?"

"What is it?" he asked.

"That she recognizes the park."

"I took her here last night."

Jordan shook her head. "She means from years ago. Her siblings frequented the park and the waterfront."

Harry scanned the area, not sure what he was looking for, but he had that weird feeling that he was being watched. When he didn't notice anyone looking at them, he gestured at the building. "Let's go in."

His heartbeat raced at the notion of going inside such a small structure, but he clenched his jaw against his claustrophobia and put one foot in front of the other.

Thankfully, the interior of the tower was larger than it appeared from outside. A spiral staircase in the center of the open room led to an upper floor. Historical displays lined all the walls, and green footprints on the floor marked the sequence for visitors.

"It's a timeline of the town's history." Jordan picked up the cat and carried her to the first exhibit. "Three families set out from Manchester to Barbados...blah, blah, blah...ran into a strong storm that pushed them off course. The storm-damaged ship eventually limped along the Florida coast but sank in more heavy winds just offshore in a hook-shaped harbor. Most of the passengers survived, but at least two perished."

Harry read the next in the series of plaques, and in the interest of time, paraphrased it. "Infighting led to each of the families claiming their own large parcels in the newly established town of Cat's Paw Cove. The Wilshire family built their settlement close to the harbor, the Bell family established themselves just to the south, and the Harrisons went west to the high ground of what is today known as Seaside Hills. Years later, a Wilshire married a Harrison, effectively merging the two great families." He rubbed his chin. "I feel as if I've heard this story before."

Jordan sucked in a breath. "Is something coming back to you?"

"Could be." Moving to the next display, he continued reading about the town's history. "Lawrence Harrison and his new wife, Matilda Wilshire Harrison, forged a partnership with the Yamasee people, a multiethnic confederation of Native Americans. Together, the natives and settlers grew the town and successfully defended it against the frequent pirate attacks. The Harrison family established a network of trading posts throughout the region. They built Sherwood House in 1759 (named after the breed of cats said to have come to Florida on the ship that carried the original families). The mansion was a family residence, which also covertly served as a safe haven for escaped slaves from the colonies of Georgia and South Carolina."

"Fascinating!" Jordan craned her neck to look up the staircase. "Looks like the exhibit continues on the second level."

They followed the green footprints up the narrow stairs to three final episodes of the town's saga.

Jordan read the verbiage. "Over the next hundred years, members of both the Wilshire and Harrison family laid claims to Sherwood House, which by then, encompassed a huge parcel of valuable, water-accessible property. In 1962 part of the home was opened for tours by a local preservation society."

Harry continued. "Today, Sherwood House is on the National Register of Historic Homes and is still owned by descendants of the Harrison and Wilshire families. The sprawling estate is also home to a large population of Sherwood cats, most of which are white with brown or grey 'masks' around their eyes."

Harry and Jordan gasped in unison.

Jordan cradled Kitty in her arms. "Are you a Sherwood?" She met Harry's stare. "She says that she is."

Harry studied the photograph next to the plaque. A group of about a dozen people stood on the porch of what was apparently the Sherwood House. Several cats could also be seen in the portrait—all of which bore a strong resemblance to Kitty. He moved closer for a better look. One of the people looked a lot like a younger version of the woman he'd seen at Coquina Castle. And there was something familiar about that porch, and the house itself.

A wave of nausea stormed through him. A headache stabbed behind his eyes. He stumbled onto a small bench in the center of the room.

"Are you all right?" Jordan asked him.

Closing his eyes for a moment, he found himself in a large room with soaring ceilings and a grand staircase.

"You'll do as you're told!" a woman's angry voice ordered.

But who was she?

"Harry?" Jordan touched his arm. "What's going on?"

"I'm not sure." He looked at the portrait again. "I've been inside that house."

"You have?"

A distant memory flashed in his mind. A strong hand slapping his cheek; shouted curses.

Chills rolled over his skin. "Sherwood House," he said. "I was there. Something terrible happened there." He was sure of it. And he needed to find out what.

CHAPTER TEN

Jordan took a left at the sign for the Sherwood House, but as soon as she drove past the imposing gates, she was sure that referring to the estate as a 'house' was the understatement of the century. "Holy cow!" Huge oaks and even a few willow trees lined the road leading to the mansion. The property reminded Jordan of grand southern plantations like those she'd seen in the movies.

Harry sat up taller in the passenger seat, and even Kitty seemed taken by the view. The cat set her front paws on the dashboard and trilled. "I'm guessing that this place is familiar to you, Kitty."

It is, the cat silently replied. *I lived here with my brothers and sisters. We went to the park a lot, too.*

Jordan told Harry what the feline had said. "What about you?" she asked Harry. "Do you recognize it here?" She turned left into the visitor lot and parked the car under a stately laurel oak.

Harry's knuckles were white as he gripped the armrest. Beads of sweat rolled down the side of his face. "I've definitely been here before. But I have the feeling that something happened to me in that house." Tiny muscles around his jaw ticked.

She swallowed hard and grasped his arm. "Hey, it's all right."

Taking her hand, he brought it to his lips and kissed her fingers. "Thanks for being here."

"Of course." She desperately wanted to help Harry — not only to recover his memory — but also to find out who'd kidnapped him four years ago. He'd never be safe if they didn't figure out who was after him. On a purely selfish level, she hoped that when he stepped into his former shoes, he'd still want her.

Jordan attached Kitty's leash to the harness. "Ready?" she asked Harry.

Throwing her a wink, he started up the path toward the house.

A large maze sat just to the right of the mansion. The hedges were easily ten feet tall. On the left side, the formal English garden bloomed with purple lavender, vibrant marigolds, and deep red mums. Jordan marveled at the imposing columns on either side of the long porch. Two cats that looked a lot like Kitty sunbathed on the floorboards. Jordan picked up Kitty and tucked the cat under her arm. "Do you know them?" she asked her.

No. They must be new here.

"She doesn't," Jordan told Harry.

Harry pointed to a sign next to the double doors. "It's open to the public." He

153

held open one of the doors and Jordan walked in ahead of him.

"Whoa." Jordan had only seen homes this grand in the movies and on TV. A giant crystal chandelier hung from the soaring ceiling of the foyer, and the artwork on the walls reminded Jordan of those in an art museum she'd visited in Miami. In the center of the room, an ornate vase filled with calla lilies sat in the center of an antique table that was probably worth more than Mallory's new house. A set of French doors off the foyer opened to a gift shop.

She followed Harry into the store, which resembled others Jordan had visited in historic homes in Savannah and Charleston. A bookcase held a small assortment of historical titles, and there was a rotating rack with postcards near the glass display case.

"Good afternoon," said a seventy-ish woman with white hair teased within an inch of its life. "We don't have scheduled tours on Sundays, but you're welcome to walk around the house on your own. Please mind the roped off areas and don't sit on any of the furniture."

Harry stepped over to the old-time cash register and took out his wallet. "Two, please."

The woman widened her eyes at him but quickly recovered. She cleared her throat. "That'll be fourteen dollars."

Harry gave her a twenty-dollar bill. Had he noticed the clerk's strange reaction to seeing him?

With trembling fingers, the woman handed Harry his change. "You can download an app for a guided tour on your phone. Look up Sherwood House Tour."

He thanked her. "How twenty-first century."

The clerk ignored his comment and walked away.

"I'll do it." Jordan took out her cell and found the application.

"Let's just walk through for now," Harry said. "I want to get a feel for this place. We can listen to the tour later."

"Of course." She slipped Kitty inside the backpack then strode with Harry into a large parlor off the foyer. Portraits of men and women in seventeenth and eighteenth-century clothing hung on the walls. Several of the subjects had sea-green eyes very similar to Harry's. A chill rolled over her skin. "Do you notice anything about some of these people?"

"I sure do." He read a description under one of the paintings. "Lawrence and Matilda Harrison."

Look at the last one, Kitty told Jordan.

Jordan moved to the most contemporary-looking portrait, which showed a couple in their late thirties with a

155

small boy. Something about the child seemed familiar. His hair was blond, but those eyes...could it be? She read the description aloud. "Allen and Jennifer Harrison with son, Sawyer."

Harry came over and stared up at the painting. He swayed for a moment, so Jordan grasped his arm. "I know them," he muttered.

"Who are they?"

He grasped the velvet rope in front of them. "They're my parents."

Jordan touched his arm. "Are you sure?"

Frowning, he shook his head. "It's still fuzzy. Let's get out of here."

"Are you sure you don't want to see the rest of the mansion?" Jordan asked as she put his cat in the back seat.

Shaking his head, he opened the passenger door for her. "Another time. Mind if I drive?"

Jordan fished in her purse until she found the keys and handed them over. "Go for it."

As he drove off the property, he gripped the steering wheel. "I have to find my parents."

"Right." She buckled her seatbelt. "Someone must know them if they're part of the town's founding family."

"We need to find a town directory. Could it be that simple?"

"Since the town hall is closed, maybe one of the businesses has a local phone book."

"Right."

They passed Purry's, and she heard Harry's stomach growl.

"I'm starving," he said. "Why don't we stop for a bite? I'm sure all the restaurants have a phone book."

Jordan slid closer and set her hand on his thigh. "I have a request."

"Yeah?"

"I'd like to eat at a place I saw last night. It's off Whiskers Lane, just up the road."

"Sure," he said.

Jordan patted her lap for Kitty to come up to the front. "You're going to have to stay in the backpack," she told the feline.

Give me a treat.

"Whatever it takes." Jordan opened the foil pouch and gave the animal what she'd requested.

Harry took the carrier, and they strode toward Calico Court. The soothing sound of falling water drew her like a magnet down the alleyway into the charming courtyard.

"This is nice," Harry commented. "Reminds me of Nocturne Falls. We're not really dressed for such a fancy restaurant, though." He tipped his chin toward Medici.

Jordan hooked his arm and pointed to Cove Cat Café. "This is where I want to go."

Understanding registered in his expression. "Ah ha. I shouldn't be surprised." He opened the glass door for her, and she went inside.

Breathing in the heavenly aromas of strong coffee, and fresh-baked pastry, Jordan sighed with pleasure. Her mouth watered as she joined the line at the long counter and took in the variety of confections and croissant sandwiches inside the glass display cases. "Wow. These all look amazing."

Take me into the playroom, Kitty implored.

As Jordan waited for their turn to order, she glanced through the large window that separated the cat area from the café. "After we get our food we'll go over there," she told the cat. But she'd have to ask whoever was in charge before letting Kitty loose with the other cats.

"Hmm?" Harry said.

She relayed Kitty's request to him.

"Hi, may I help you?" A lanky brunette with a deep olive complexion smoothed a short dreadlock off of her forehead.

Jordan pointed to a croissant stuffed with Brie in the case. "I'd like that sandwich and a cinnamon latte. And admission into the cat room."

"Just double that," Harry told the barista.

The young woman handed another customer a tray with coffee, and a pastry then punched a few buttons on the register screen. "It'll be a few minutes if that's okay. I'm all by myself here, and my adoptions manager is getting married and moving away next week."

"No problem," Jordan assured her.

Harry handed the woman his credit card. "Would you happen to have a local phone directory?"

"Sure, give me a sec." She gave back Harry's card then plated the sandwiches.

Jordan pulled a few napkins from a dispenser. "Would it be all right if he let out his cat in the playroom? We've got a leash for her, but she'll behave."

The barista glanced at the backpack. "Sure, but I'd prefer if you'd keep her leashed." She handed Harry a tray.

"No problem," Harry told her.

The woman disappeared into a back room for a moment before returning. She gave Jordan a small phone book. "Here you go."

"Thanks," she said. "I'll return it before we leave."

After Harry got their drinks, they went into the cat room and set their order on a bistro table in the corner.

Jordan attached Kitty's leash and took her out of the carrier. Several cats came over.

Hi, who are you? An orange and white tabby sniffed Kitty's nose.

159

A Siamese mix rubbed against Jordan's shin. *Want to play?*

Jordan hung her sweater over the back of her chair. "After I eat."

While Harry thumbed through the phone book, Jordan watched the cats chase toy mice, and climb the carpet-covered cat trees and the high ledges on the walls. The atmosphere was so warm and cozy. If she and Harry weren't on an important mission, she'd have loved to stay at the café all day.

Harry set his sandwich down and frowned. "Alan and Jennifer Harrison aren't listed, but..." His lips flattened to a tight line.

She sipped her coffee. "But what?"

"Sawyer Harrison is listed."

"The son?" She met his stare. "You."

New lines fanned out from the corners of Harry's eyes. "It very well could be. This phonebook is four years old."

Jordan checked the listing then typed the address and phone number into her phone. "Let's check it out."

Harry took Kitty with him as he went to return the phone book to the barista.

Jordan noticed a striped tabby sitting under one of the tables. She went over and crouched down to pet the cat. "Hi sweetie, I'm Jordan."

The feline lifted his head for a moment. *Hi.*

160

"Are you okay?" Jordan asked it.

My tooth hurts. I can't eat anything, but I'm hungry. The tabby laid his head down again.

"Ready?"

Glancing up at Harry, Jordan nodded. "Give me a moment." She threw away her trash then returned to the counter.

The barista was taking an order. Glancing at Jordan, she said, "I'll be right with you."

"Sure."

The woman handed the customer his coffee as she answered the phone. "Cove Cat Café, this is Luna." She nodded and furrowed her brow. "I see...mm-hmm. Right. Thanks, Dr. Anderson." After she hung up, the woman looked at Jordan. "Did you need something?"

Jordan swallowed. Would the barista think she was crazy? All Jordan could do was hope not. "The striped tabby with the purple collar isn't feeling well."

The woman raised an eyebrow. "I know. That was the vet on the phone returning my call. He's going to see Tiger in the morning."

"Tiger," Jordan repeated. "He's got a toothache. It's why he isn't eating."

Luna stilled. "How'd you know that he hasn't been eating?"

Jordan shrugged. "Lucky guess. But trust me. The problem is a dental one."

161

Widening her eyes, the woman slowly nodded. "O...kay."

So what if Luna thought Jordan was crazy. As long as the cat got care soon, Jordan didn't mind. Before they left, Jordan waved goodbye to her new feline friends. She offered up a silent wish that someday she'd be able to visit again when she had more time. "Where to?" she asked Harry.

He opened the passenger door of her car for her. "Sawyer Harrison's house."

"Your old home?" she asked.

Harry's chest expanded with a breath. "Time will tell."

CHAPTER ELEVEN

"We're almost there." Jordan looked up from the navigation app on her phone. "The house should be up here on the right."

Harry swallowed past the dryness in his throat as he drove toward a large Spanish-style home with a terracotta roof on a bluff overlooking the Atlantic.

Jordan covered his hand with hers. "Well?"

"I'm not sure." His heart thundered in his chest. Maybe the house had been his at one time, but clearly, someone else was living there now. A stone fountain in the yard was running, and the grass had been recently mowed.

"Let's go knock on the door." Jordan opened her door. "Ready?"

No. "Sure." He opened the car windows to give his cat air. "Be right back, Kitty." Steeling himself, he headed up the walk toward the stone porch. Knowing Jordan was by his side gave him the confidence to face whatever lay behind that arched doorway.

Jordan rang the bell.

Harry inhaled the salty sea air and let the soothing sound of the waves calm his nerves.

After a minute or so, a middle-aged blond opened the door. "Yes?"

Glancing past the woman, he saw a staircase with shelves built into the triangular wall underneath.

I built those shelves.

Goosebumps rose on his skin.

"Um...hello," Jordan said. "We were...um..."

"I used to live here," Harry blurted out.

The blond raised an eyebrow. "Oh?" She paled as she took a backward step and grasped the doorknob. "What do you want?"

Jordan cleared her throat. "Would it be okay if we looked around?"

The woman shook her head. "No, I don't think so." She started to shut the door."

"Wait," Harry implored. "Who sold this place?"

She eyed him for several seconds. "I rent it, actually. My landlady is Angelica Jespers." With that, she closed the door.

"Angelica Jespers," he murmured.

Jordan typed on her phone as they returned to the car. "I'm Googling her."

Harry started the motor. Movement nearby caught his eye. A black sedan sped past them. "That's the same car that was following me back in Nocturne Falls."

Gasping, Jordan buckled her seatbelt and held Kitty on her lap. "Are you sure?"

He took off after the other vehicle. "Ninety-nine percent sure."

The sedan raced along the narrow, winding road, picking up more and more speed. Harry stayed on the driver's tail.

When the other car rounded a curve too quickly, it skidded off the road and crashed in a sandy ditch. Harry pulled over. "Stay in the car," he told Jordan. "And call for help."

"Be careful."

Harry got out, opened the trunk, and grabbed a tire iron. Then he started toward the sedan. Dark tint obscured his view into the vehicle, but when he walked closer, he saw the silhouette of a man slumped at the wheel. Smoke rose from under the hood.

Harry pulled open the door and dragged the unconscious man away.

Jordan descended the slope toward him. "Help is on the way."

"Move your car," he told Jordan. "The sedan could be leaking gasoline."

Sirens wailed in the distance, coming toward them. Harry felt the man's neck and found a pulse. Too bad the guy wasn't conscious. Hopefully, he'd be all right and could tell them why he'd been stalking them.

A police car screeched to a stop a few yards from Jordan's vehicle. A firetruck arrived moments after, and three firemen jumped out. Two headed to the crashed sedan, and one came over to tend to the driver.

The cop strode toward Harry. When he was a few feet away, the brown-haired officer looked at Harry and gasped. The man drew his weapon and trained it on Harry. "You! Put your hands up where I can see them, and get down on your knees."

"No! It wasn't his fault." Jordan closed the distance to Harry and wrapped her arms around him. "The other driver has been following him. That man even broke into the house where I'm staying."

"Step away from him, ma'am," the officer warned.

She shook her head. "You can't do this."

Harry eased her back. "It'll be okay." But he knew it would never be okay again. All of his worst fears about his past were true. Whatever sins he'd committed back then, he'd have to pay for them now. He kneeled on the ground, and as the handcuffs clicked around his wrists, he resigned himself to whatever fate he'd earned during a life he couldn't even recall.

"Embezzlement," Sheriff RJ Higgins told Jordan when she arrived at the police station. "The money that your boyfriend stole nearly bankrupted this town's oldest and dearest landmark, the Sherwood House."

When the police had arrived at the scene of the accident a little while ago, and they'd immediately arrested Harry, Jordan had wondered if Harry had indeed been a criminal in his former life. But it had only taken her a split second to realize that the cops had to be wrong about him. Sure, she had a history of unwittingly falling for bad boys, but she knew in her heart of hearts that Harry was a good man, and always had been. The sheriff was mistaken.

She unclenched her fists and drew a calming breath. "Someone kidnapped Harry four years ago. They tried to kill him, but miraculously he survived. Only he had no memory of anything that happened before he came to."

The sheriff lowered himself into his desk chair and folded his arms over his muscular chest. "Yeah, he claims that he's had a convenient case of amnesia for the past four years. That's about as implausible as aliens landing a spaceship in the middle of Wilshire Park."

Having lived in Nocturne Falls for more than a year, Jordan knew such a thing was in fact, possible, but saying so would only weaken her case. "Why haven't you questioned the driver of the black sedan yet? You have to believe me, Sheriff. I'm sure he's the one who broke in and nearly killed Harry a few days ago in Nocturne Falls, Georgia."

Higgins shrugged. "I'd love to hear what he's got to say. Unfortunately, he's still unconscious. One of my officers is with him, though. Deputy Fuller will let me know when he comes out of it. And your boyfriend's name is Sawyer Harrison, not Harry Hill."

Jordan paced the floor in the sheriff's small office. "When can I speak to Harry...er...Sawyer?"

The sheriff glanced past Jordan and called to the middle-aged receptionist in the outer office. "Delores, has our prisoner been booked yet?"

Booked? Jordan conjured an image of poor Harry being fingerprinted and thrown into a tiny, dank dungeon. Her blood ran cold.

"I'll check, boss." The brunette picked up her phone and spoke into it too quietly for Jordan to hear. After a minute or so, she hung up. "Pete says he's finished processing the prisoner."

Sheriff Higgins stood up and gestured for Jordan to follow him. "Come on."

Jordan asked the receptionist if she'd mind watching Kitty for a few minutes.

The woman's face lit up as she held out her arms for the carrier. "I'd be thrilled."

Sheriff Higgins led Jordan to the back of the building. He unlocked a metal door and ushered Jordan into a concrete room that was divided into three jail cells with too-bright fluorescent lighting.

Harry was lying on a cot in the middle cell, she ran over and gripped the bars. "Are you all right?"

He sat up but the deep lines creasing his brow, and his sagging shoulders assured her that he was anything but. "I'm sorry I let you down, Jordan."

She swallowed past the golfball-sized lump in her throat. "I'm going to get you out of here."

Harry merely shook his head. "Cut your losses. I'm not worth it. Will you keep my cat for me?"

"Only if you promise me that you won't give up on yourself. Because *I* never will." How was she going to get him out of there? She didn't have bail money, not that she had any idea how much that would be. There had to be something she could do, someone she could call.

A thought occurred to her. "What about your parents?" Turning to the sheriff, she asked, "Do you know where Har...I mean Sawyer's parents live. I'm sure they would help him."

Higgins blanched. He looked from Jordan to Sawyer then back again. "You really don't know?"

"Know what?" Harry asked.

After several beats, Higgins removed his hat and stepped closer to the cell door. "Your folks died almost twenty years ago, Sawyer."

Harry/Sawyer hung his head. Tiny muscles around his jaw ticked. "How?"

The sheriff muttered a curse under his breath. "Boating accident. You were the only survivor."

Sawyer squeezed his eyes shut for a long moment. "I had no idea."

Jordan's heart broke for him. She cared about Sawyer, and he'd rescued her more than once. Being strong was the best way she could help him. "Sheriff Higgins, you said that Sawyer is accused of embezzling money from the Sherwood House. Wasn't it Sawyer's family that owned the place?"

Higgins nodded. "Several descendants, including Sawyer, hold shares. After his parents passed away, his aunt and uncle raised Sawyer, and they managed his share along with theirs." He cleared his throat. "In fact, it was that same aunt who brought Sawyer's crime to light, which couldn't have been easy for her."

Sawyer narrowed his eyes at the sheriff. "What's her name?"

"Angelica Jespers."

Why did that ring a bell? Jordan had heard someone mention her, but who? Then it hit her. The woman who was renting Sawyer's old house had said that her landlady was Angelica Jespers. Jordan swallowed a gasp.

Sawyer slid her a glance then looked at Sheriff Higgins. "What about the driver of the black sedan? Do you know his name?"

Higgins brushed a hand over his chin. "Not yet. He didn't have any identification on him. The car is registered to a thug out of Atlanta."

"Is he Eastern European?" Sawyer asked.

The sheriff lifted an eyebrow. "As a matter of fact, yes. He's Czech."

Harry's lip compressed to a tight line. "Who took control of my stake in the Sherwood House after I...left town?"

"Angelica." Higgins frowned.

"What is it, Sheriff?" Jordan asked.

"My predecessor, the previous sheriff, was Parnell Jespers, Angelica's late husband. He died two years ago of a heart attack."

Sawyer tightened his fingers around the bars. "Did you ever consider that the Jespers were actually the ones who stole that money?"

Higgins rubbed his temples. "I wasn't the sheriff then, and it wasn't my case."

"Perhaps that case should be reopened," Jordan suggested. She recalled something Kitty had told her. "Sheriff Higgins, does your department have any vans?"

"One. We rarely use it anymore, though. Why?"

"Does it have stripes?" Sawyer asked him.

"Sure, blue and yellow, just like the rest of our vehicles."

Kitty had described the van as striped. Jordan's heart thundered in her chest. But how could she make the sheriff believe something that a cat had conveyed to her? "Sheriff, can you question Angelica Jespers?"

"Angelica Jespers is the closest thing this town has to high society." He held up his palms. "What would I ask her? If she and her dead husband tried to kill her only nephew?"

"Yes!" Although anyone who'd do such a thing would surely deny it. The sheriff's hands were tied, but Jordan's weren't.

"I can't believe this?" Sawyer clenched his fists. "So Sheriff Jespers—my uncle—investigated the trumped up charges against me, charges that his wife corroborated? No impropriety there."

Higgins huffed out a breath. "The previous sheriff's administration was corrupt. He was under investigation by the FDLE when he suffered a fatal heart attack."

"FDLE?" Jordan repeated.

"Florida Department of Law Enforcement," Higgins explained.

Sawyer stood taller. "What do I need to do to get out of here, Sheriff?"

Higgins scratched his head. "Normally you'd have your first appearance before the judge tomorrow morning. But Judge Parnell is my fishing buddy, and I can call in a favor and ask him to set your bail this afternoon."

"Thank you, Sheriff," Sawyer said.

"I'm not sure why I believe your story," Higgins said. "But I do."

Jordan drew a relieved breath. Somehow, she was going to prove that Sawyer wasn't the criminal he'd been made out to be.

CHAPTER TWELVE

After Sawyer paid his thousand-dollar bail, he collected his personal property then walked out of the office.

Jordan stood under a streetlamp outside with his cat in her arms. She closed the distance to him.

He held her for a long time, drinking in her sweet scent, feeling the comfort of her warmth. "You have no idea how much I missed you."

"Actually, I do." She raised up on her tiptoes to kiss him. "My sister's going to take care of the Tuckers' cats again tonight. Mal's a lifesaver. I don't know what I'd have done without her."

Sawyer held Jordan at arms' length. "I'll understand if you want to go back to Nocturne Falls without me. But I've got to stay here until I work out this situation."

"I understand." Her lips bunched to one side. "I have to honor my commitment to Mrs. Tucker, but we'll think of something."

"Did you find out where Angelica lives?"

She nodded as she unlocked her car with the key fob. "It's almost ten o'clock, though. Shouldn't we wait until morning to go talk to her?"

"Definitely." He opened Jordan's car door for her then took Kitty and put her in the back seat. "Tonight I want to scope out her house, see if anything there jogs my memory."

Jordan navigated while Sawyer drove along a winding road that hugged the coast. They turned into Seaside Hills. The subdivision didn't look familiar to him. Around each bend, they passed one grand Victorian home after another.

"Holy moly." Jordan gestured toward a mansion that dwarfed the Tuckers' home by comparison. "I think that's it. You grew up here?"

He pulled over next to a high wrought iron fence that surrounded the property. Large gas lanterns marked the entrance which, unfortunately, didn't look familiar to him. "I have no idea."

"According to Sheriff Higgins, you lived with the Jespers from the time you were twelve years old." Jordan sat up taller. "Did you hear that?"

Sawyer listened. A dog barked in the distance.

"Sounds like a Doberman." She frowned. "How can you tell from so far away?"

She leaned her head against the headrest and pursed her lips. "I think it's sort of like how people can discern different accents.

COURTING THE CAT WHISPERER

Certain breeds of dogs—and even cats to a lesser degree—have characteristic traits."

If she were right, they wouldn't be able to get near the house to even peer in the windows. He didn't much care for dogs, especially big ones. For some reason, they made him nervous. "Too bad it's not a chihuahua."

She raised an eyebrow. "You'd be surprised how effective some small breeds are as watchdogs. They can make one heck of a racket."

"What if you ask the dog to be quiet?"

"I might not be able to convince it to do that."

He was so close. His whole body vibrated with anticipation. He needed to go see the house and try to remember something of his former life. "You stay here," he told Jordan. "I'm going to poke around outside."

"What about the dog?" Jordan unbuckled her seatbelt. "I'm coming with you. You'll need me there if you run into a Dobie."

By now, he knew her well enough to be sure that she wouldn't stay put if she didn't want to. "Promise me you'll stay behind me, and that you'll run back to the car if there's trouble."

She huffed. "Fine." Easing open her door, she stopped. "I've got an idea. A lot of dogs love cat treats. And we happen to have a pouch in the glovebox."

"You're a genius." He gave her a quick kiss. "Safety first, Jordan."

"Absolutely." After slipping a few treats into her pocket, she got out of the car.

"We'll be right back, Kitty." Jeez, was he really conversing with his cat? Now that he knew she understood his words, why not?

Taking Jordan's hand, he headed toward the circular driveway. They crouched down just before the opening. An older model Toyota was parked near the house.

"Strange that someone with such a fancy home would drive a car like that," Jordan said quietly.

"I'd lay odds that it doesn't belong to Angelica." Sawyer tipped his chin at the three-car garage.

"Ah ha. You're probably right."

Sawyer scoped out the property. If they stayed close to the outer perimeter until they reached the garage, they'd avoid most of the landscape lighting. "Follow me," he said. They were almost at the garage when the front door of the house opened.

Two silhouetted female figures stepped out to the porch.

Sawyer pulled Jordan around the side of the garage and held a finger to his lips.

Jordan nodded.

"Remember our bargain," one of the women said. "Keep your mouth shut and everything will be fine."

"I have for all these years."

Sawyer held his breath. He knew that voice.

"Then how did he find out? This is all your fault, Gladys."

The door slammed shut.

Jordan tightened her grip on his hand. Had she recognized the voice as well?

A minute or so later, a car motor sputtered twice before turning over.

Sawyer ventured a glance at the woman behind the wheel as she drove past. All he could make out was her white hair. He felt the heat of Jordan's breath on the back of his neck.

"Did you see who that was?" she whispered. "It was the clerk from the Sherwood House."

"Are you sure?"

"Positive. Didn't you notice that giant white beehive?"

Jordan was right. That was why her voice sounded familiar. "What do you think that conversation was about?"

Sawyer's phone vibrated in his pocket, but he wasn't in a position to have a conversation. He checked the call log, and when he saw Cat's Paw Cove Sheriff in the display, he showed it to Jordan. "Let's go back to the car. This could be important."

When he phoned the number, Sheriff Higgins answered.

"What's up, Sheriff?" Sawyer asked.

"I thought you'd want to know," Higgins replied. "The driver of the other car has regained consciousness. I'm on my way to St. John's County General now."

Sawyer checked his watch. "I'll meet you there."

"Oh no you won't," the sheriff replied. "I'll arrest you if you attempt to influence his testimony in any way."

"Fine," Sawyer ground out. "Would you at least tell me what he says?"

"If I can." The sheriff disconnected.

"Did you hear all of that?" he asked Jordan.

She frowned. "Yup. What now?"

"Until we find out what the guy in the hospital has to say, we're dead in the water." He glanced at the house. The light in a second-story window turned off.

Jordan slid lower in the seat. "He might not say anything, which puts us right back to square one."

Nervous energy pulsed through him. "I'm too antsy to wait. I'm going to try to look in the windows."

"Let's go."

He touched her knee. "I won't put you in any more danger."

She smiled, but her eyes glistened. "I care about you, too. My life is a whole lot more exciting since I met you."

He had to laugh at that. "I guess that's one way to look at it."

"Ready?"

Giving her leg a quick squeeze, he smoothed her silky hair. Yeah, he did care about her. Despite his vow to hold back until he knew more about his past, his feelings for Jordan had grown. He only prayed that whatever they discovered about his past, made him worthy of her.

They circled around the house to the back, which wasn't nearly as well-lit as the front. Waves crashed on the nearby shoreline, muting most other sounds.

A dog barked from inside the house. Sawyer tightened his grip on Jordan's hand.

She made the okay sign with her thumb and index finger as she moved closer to a window.

A black Doberman snarled at them from the other side of the glass.

"It's okay," Jordan said. "What's your name, fellow?" She nodded slowly, and the dog sat down.

Sawyer's pounding heart slowed a little. "You're amazing, Jordan."

"His name is Excalibur," she whispered.

Great, a dog named for a sword.

"Do you like your mistress?" Jordan asked the pooch. Then she touched a finger to the glass. "Poor baby."

"Does he know me?" Sawyer stared at the dog, racking his brain to remember the animal. "I mean, from years ago."

Jordan sighed. "You were to only one who was kind to him."

"What about Angelica's late husband?"

After several seconds, Jordan shook her head. "Excalibur says that Parnell was almost as bad as Angelica." Jordan held up her index finger at Sawyer, asking for him to wait. Several moments passed as Jordan nodded and seemed to commiserate with the dog. Finally, she gasped.

"What?"

Taking Sawyer's hand, she eased him a few feet back from the window. "Excalibur is a good listener. And he remembers overhearing his mistress and his late master arguing…a lot. He says it was many years ago."

"Okay." He steeled himself for whatever she was about to tell him.

"Angelica wanted her husband to…to kill someone."

A chill rolled over his skin. "To kill *me*?"

Jordan's lips compressed to a thin line. "The dog doesn't know, but since someone did try to kill you, they had to be talking about you."

Jordan moved closer to the window. "Excalibur, would you do me a solid and keep quiet while we look around? I promise that we aren't here to hurt your mistress." She smiled up at Sawyer. "He won't bark."

"I'm not going to break into the woman's house." Something drew his attention to the garage. "But I want to go in there."

Jordan followed his gaze. "Why?"

"I don't know. Just a feeling." A creepy one.

The side door into the garage was unlocked. The instant Sawyer stepped inside, his heart started thumping against his ribs. "I've been here before."

Jordan mated her fingers with his. "Is it the same feeling you got when you were in the Sherwood House?"

This was definitely different. "That was more...sad. Here it's more like...intense fear."

Jordan turned on her cell's flashlight app, illuminating the large, open room. Every imaginable type of tool hung on the back wall. The SUV that had sped away from Coquina Castle was parked in one of the two spaces.

"That confirms that Angelica Jespers was the woman we saw this morning at the festival," Sawyer said.

"Yup." Jordan trained her light on a small, narrow door with a padlock. "I wonder what's in there."

Sawyer's breath locked in his lungs. Nausea swirled in the pit of his belly.

"Hey." Jordan stepped in front of him. "Are you okay?"

"Not really." He scanned the tool until he found a bolt cutter. It only took him a few moments to break the lock. Head pounding, he pulled open the door. A familiar smell filled the air. He stumbled backward.

"What's wrong?" Jordan grasped his forearm. "Do you remember something?"

He could only nod as terrifying memories populated what had been a blank space inside him.

"Let me out!"

He'd slammed his fists on the door. "Please, Aunt Angelica! I promise I'll be good." Although he'd had no clue what he'd done to merit the punishment.

"Duke, attack him if he gets out," his aunt told her dog.

Duke growled on the other side of the door.

Jordan led him away from the closet to a stool. "Sit down. Tell me what's going on."

"I remember something." He sucked in a deep breath and waited for his pulse to slow.

183

"She used to lock me in there and had her German shepherd, Duke stand guard. That dog hated me, probably because Angelica told him to."

"That's horrid." Jordan crouched next to him. "She sounds like an awful woman."

He nodded. "And her husband knew what she did. He helped her." Now he understood why small, enclosed spaces bothered him so much, and why he was uncomfortable around large dogs.

His phone buzzed. When he checked it, there was a text message from Sheriff Higgins. *"Need to speak to you. Call when you get this."*

Jordan handed Sawyer one of the two cups of coffee she'd gotten from the sheriff's outer office. Heaven knew she needed something to perk her up since it was well after midnight, and she had no clue when she'd get a chance to sleep.

"Sorry to drag you folks in here so late." Sheriff Higgins leaned his elbows on his desk. "I thought you'd want to know what Boris Komisky had to say."

"The Czech?" Sawyer petted Kitty as she rubbed against his shin.

"He sang like a damn canary." Higgins tapped a folder in front of him. "Gave us everything we need to arrest your aunt."

Sawyer set down his coffee. "We learned a few things about her tonight."

"Oh?" Sheriff Higgins narrowed his eyes at Sawyer.

On second thought, maybe it wouldn't be smart to tell the top local lawman about their adventures earlier in the evening, which could be construed as breaking and entering. "Nevermind. What'd you find out?"

"Boris Komisky says he's an unlicensed Private Investigator. What he really does is anything illegal or unsavory for clients willing to pay his exorbitant fees. Mrs. Jespers has been using Boris's services for years. And apparently, so did her late husband." Higgins shook his head. "When I think about how long Parnell Jespers was sheriff of Cat's Paw Cove, and how corrupt the man was, it makes me sick to my stomach."

Sawyer knew the feeling. Hour by hour, he'd recalled more snippets from his memory—Angelica repeatedly locking him in that garage closet when he was only eleven or twelve years old, her husband beating him with a belt for no reason. "They were both awful people."

"The DA has subpoenaed all the financial records for the Sherwood House Trust," Higgins said. "What I suspect we'll learn is that Angelica mismanaged or flat out stole your money. I want to apologize for your experience here, being arrested and all. We were going on the information we had."

Sawyer digested the sheriff's apology. "I guess your administration just inherited the lies that the previous sheriff had told."

Higgins nodded. "That doesn't make it right. I hope you can forgive us. That's not what this town is all about."

"Any idea why no one here seemed to recognize me?"

Sheriff Higgins shrugged. "You were a bit of a loner. From what I've heard, you spent most of your time renovating your house."

Jordan chuckled. "That's what he does for a living in Nocturne Falls."

The sheriff grinned. "He didn't need to work back then. I believe that your parents' estate left you financially independent."

Jordan cleared her throat. "Sheriff, the woman who works in the gift shop at the Sherwood House—"

"Gladys?" Higgins interjected. "What about her?"

"She's involved in this." Jordan leveled a worried stare at Sawyer. "I mean, I suspect that she is."

The sheriff's smile faded. "Well, technically, Gladys works for Angelica."

Jordan pursed her lips for several moments before speaking. "I overheard the two women talking. Angelica said that they had a bargain and that if Gladys kept her mouth shut, everything would be okay."

Higgins scrubbed a hand over his face. "I'll bring Gladys in for questioning."

"Is she a friend of yours?" Sawyer asked.

"Not exactly. Gladys was my Sunday school teacher when I was a kid. I've always liked her." He drew a long breath. "I'll bring her in for questioning in the morning."

Sunday school teacher or not, the woman was probably complicit in a crime. If she was, she had to be brought to justice.

Higgins stood. "If y'all need a place to stay tonight, the town keeps a suite available at The Breakers, over near the beach. We usually put up visiting dignitaries, but you're welcome to use it."

Jordan gave Sawyer a discreet thumbs up.

When they walked through the glass doors into the hotel's lobby a little while later, Jordan gasped. "Nice!"

Sawyer had to agree. And their suite was just as opulent as the rest of the place, with a wide balcony overlooking the ocean, a huge living room with a full bar and a projection TV, and two bedrooms — each with a private bath and a whirlpool tub. But he was too exhausted to do anything but fall into the king-sized bed and shut his eyes.

He'd had one hell of a day. Tomorrow would truly be the first day of the rest of his life.

A knock at his bedroom door surprised him. "Come in," he told Jordan.

She entered wearing those adorable cat and dog pajamas, looking like the sexiest thing he'd ever seen.

He wouldn't have to wait until morning to start living his life after all.

CHAPTER THIRTEEN

Jordan paced the sheriff's outer office as she waited for Sheriff Higgins to finish questioning Gladys Peters. When the air conditioner kicked on, she rubbed her arms. "I didn't see my sweater in the car," she said.

Sawyer looked up at her from the vinyl couch. "Did you leave it at the hotel?"

"Maybe." Her mind had been on other things this morning when they'd checked out, like how her muscles were a little sore from using her body in all sorts of delicious ways. Even though she'd been incredibly tired when they'd settled into their suite at The Breakers, somehow, she'd found the energy to show Sawyer just how much she liked him.

He stood up and attached his cat's leash to her harness. "I'm going to take Kitty for a walk."

But before he'd made it to the door, Gladys came out of the sheriff's office. Her face was streaked with tears.

She approached Sawyer and hung her head. "I'm so sorry that I didn't have the courage to speak up years ago."

Lines fanned out from the corners of Sawyer's eyes. "Why didn't you?"

Gladys's shoulders stooped. "I tried. I wrote you an anonymous note several years ago and left it in your mailbox. Did you get it?"

His eyes widened. "I might have."

"The letter you had on you when you woke in the woods?" Jordan asked him.

He sat down and scratched his head. "Yes, that's what it was. I remember now. It was handwritten but formal. It started with 'Dear Mr. Harrison.' Which is why I thought my name was Harry."

"It got wet," Jordan explained to the older woman. "Most of the ink washed off."

Gladys sat next to Sawyer. "I can't apologize enough. I told you in the letter that Angelica had been skimming money from your share of the Sherwood House Trust for years. You see, I was the bookkeeper for the charity."

Sheriff Higgins came over. "The DA's office will be in touch with you soon, Gladys."

She cringed. "I understand."

Higgins touched the woman's shoulder. "Try not to worry too much."

After Gladys left, Sheriff Higgins told Sawyer and Jordan that the DA had offered Gladys immunity from prosecution if she testified against Angelica. She'd agreed.

"What about my dear old aunt?" Sawyer's nostrils flared. "I hope they'll throw the book at her."

Higgins nodded. "That's the plan. My deputies arrested her a little while ago. Anything you can recall will help."

"My memories are returning in bits and pieces."

The sheriff crouched to pet Kitty. "The DA suggested that we bring in a psychologist who specializes in trauma and memory loss. He'll be arriving in town next week from New York. I hope you'll stick around for that."

Sawyer met Jordan's stare. "We've got to get back to Nocturne Falls," he said. "But I'll come back for that."

Jordan hated the idea of leaving Cat's Paw Cove, but she had responsibilities back in Nocturne Falls. She couldn't expect her sister to keep taking care of the Tuckers' cats.

As they left the station, she shivered at the cool morning air. She opened the trunk of her car and rummaged through it in search of her sweater, but it wasn't there. "I wish I knew where my sweater was."

"When did you last wear it?" Sawyer asked.

She racked her brain to remember. "The cat café. I bet it's there."

Sawyer offered his hand. "Let's go."

Excitement bubbled inside Jordan. She'd been hoping for a chance to return to the café. She adored the atmosphere, and she really liked Luna, the barista. But walking hand in hand with Sawyer, she realized that it was more than the prospect of visiting the café again. She hadn't been this happy in a very long time. And that was all on Sawyer. But what if he decided to return to Cat's Paw Cove? Would their fledgling romance survive the difficulties of a long-distance relationship?

"I've been thinking," Sawyer said.

"Yeah? About what?"

They waited for the traffic light to change before crossing the street.

"I'm remembering a lot of what happened to me here. My aunt locked me in that dark closet in her garage for days at a time. As soon as I was old enough to move out, I did. I bought my own house on the outskirts of town. And I was a hermit."

Jordan's chest constricted. "I understand that after all you'd suffered at your aunt's hands."

"My memory is still a lot like a piece of Swiss cheese, all full of holes and blank spaces."

They turned into the courtyard toward the cat café. The calming sound of the water fountain and the sweet floral aromas surrounded Jordan like a cozy silk shawl. She wished that she could spend more time there.

"I'm also beginning to recall things from before my parents' death, lots of great memories."

Jordan gulped. "Does that mean you're considering moving back here?" Not that she could blame him if he wanted to live there. If she could, she'd have made the same decision.

Sawyer exhaled. "I have my business back in Nocturne Falls, and you." He stopped walking and faced her.

Her heart fluttered.

"Sawyer? Sawyer Harrison, is that you?" A tall woman with blue hair ran over and practically leaped into Sawyer's arms.

Jordan backed away. Who was the beauty queen? His wife? Girlfriend? Tears stung behind Jordan's eyes but she clenched her jaw to keep herself from crying.

The brunette kissed Sawyer's cheeks in turn. "I'd almost given up hope of ever seeing you again." She hooked her arms around his neck and buried her face against his chest.

Jordan couldn't take any more. She slipped inside the café and sank onto a chair.

Luna squealed as she approached her. "You're back! I didn't know how to reach you."

Jordan managed a nod. "So you found my sweater?"

"Hmm?" Understanding registered in the barista's expression. "Oh, yes. We did."

Jordan wiped a tear from her face. "Great, thanks."

"But that's not why I wanted to talk to you." Luna sat at the table with her and called over her shoulder at the dark-haired young man behind the counter. "Leo, I'm taking my break now."

He gave her a thumbs up as he poured coffee into a blender.

Luna turned back around. "So I wanted to tell you that Tiger does have an issue with his tooth, an abscess. He's at the vet's now."

Jordan tried to banish the image of that woman kissing Sawyer. She shut her eyes for a moment then focused on Luna. "Who?"

"The cat, Tiger. You told me that he wasn't eating because there was a problem with his tooth. And there is." Luna clasped her hands on the table and leaned in closer. "What I don't understand is how you knew that."

Jordan sat up taller in her seat. "Well, I...like I told you yesterday, it was a lucky guess."

Luna's lips bunched to one side. She lowered her voice. "Or perhaps, Tiger told you."

She looked into Luna's deep brown eyes. If only Jordan's telepathic gifts worked on humans. "I...um..."

"You read his mind?" Luna raised an eyebrow. "I've heard of people who have that power. And I'm very interested."

"Interested?"

The other woman smiled. "What's wrong with me? You don't know me from Adam's house cat, do you?" She offered her hand. "I'm Luna Halpern. My brother Leo and I own this place." Glancing over her shoulder again, she yelled, "Leo, say hi."

"Hi." He rolled his eyes and laughed.

Jordan shook with her. "Jordan Vaughn."

"Nice to meet you, Jordan. I'll cut to the chase. We just lost our rescue manager, the person who ran the cat rescue side of things. Leo and I know the coffee house business, but neither of us is an expert in feline stuff."

"Well, I don't know if I'd call myself an expert," Jordan said. "I mean, I don't have any formal education or training."

"But you can communicate with them."

Jordan's head buzzed. So much had happened in the past few days. How was she supposed to think when Sawyer was probably right outside canoodling with that woman? "Do you have my sweater?"

"Huh?" Luna frowned. "If you left it here, it'll be in the lost and found box. Over there." She pointed to the far corner.

Jordan headed over there and plucked her sweater from the box.

"Would you at least think about it?" Luna asked.

"About what?"

"A job. I'd like you to manage the café rescue part of this place." Luna grinned, and Jordan noticed that she and Leo had the exact same smile, and their eyes were the identical shade of brown. She closed the distance between them and handed Jordan a business card. "Best way to reach me is a Facebook message. Promise me you'll let me know."

Jordan stashed the card in her purse. "Um, yeah. Sure."

"Yay!" Luna pulled her into a hug. "Sorry, I'm a total space invader, but only when I like someone." She backed away. "Can I get you a latte? On the house, of course."

Out of the corner of her eye, she glimpsed Sawyer near the fountain in the courtyard. "No thanks. I'll be in touch." When she left the café, she realized that Sawyer was talking on the phone. The woman he'd been playing kissy-face with was nowhere in sight. Good.

"Thanks, Sheriff," Sawyer said into the phone. "I appreciate it." He disconnected then met Jordan's stare. "I guess you found your sweater."

"And what did you find? Or rather, *who* found you?" She regretted the question the instant it left her mouth. "I'm sorry. It's none of my business."

Sawyer pulled her to a wrought iron bistro table and sat down with her. He set Kitty on the ground. "Of course it's your business." He started to speak, but stopped and averted his gaze. Was he nervous to tell her that the woman had meant something to him in the past? That she still did?"

Jordan braced herself for another letdown. Wasn't as if she hadn't had her heart broken before. She'd survive. "Just say it, Sawyer. I'm a big girl."

His brow creased. "It's difficult to say."

She swallowed hard.

"Her name is Martine," he finally said. "She told me a lot of things, answered many questions for me."

"Were the two of you...close?" Jordan didn't really want him to answer that. It was going to hurt too much.

"Very."

Her insides twisted.

"She works at the salon in town, Claws-N-Coifs. I think she said that she does nails."

Good for her.

Sawyer slid his chair closer. "Apparently, some people who lived here back when my parents died suspected that the boating accident that took their lives wasn't an accident at all." He pinched the bridge of his nose. "I'll speak to Sheriff

Higgins about that, but it's probably too long ago to prove anything."

"You think your aunt had something to with it?" she asked.

"That would be my guess. Maybe Angelica's late husband." Sawyer shrugged. "I wonder if Gladys knows more than she's saying."

"I'm so sorry."

"Martine also told me that my uncle, Sheriff Jespers, had a gambling problem. That was well known around town." Tiny muscles around his jaw ticked. "Martine said that I told her things about my childhood, the time after my parents died when I lived with the Jespers. I told her that they used to lock me in that closet in the garage. So my memory of that is true."

Jordan clenched her jaw to keep from crying. She squeezed Sawyer's hand. "That's so awful."

"Yeah. Martine never believed Angelica's claim that I'd run off with almost a million dollars that I'd stolen from the Sherwood House Trust. But at the time, with the sheriff being Angelica's husband, she had no recourse."

Jordan had to know what Sawyer's relationship had been with Martine. "So you two were...dating?"

Sawyer widened his eyes. "Martine and I?" He shook his head and smiled. "Martine *Harrison*? She's my cousin."

All the tension in Jordan's neck and shoulders eased. "Your cousin." That was a relief. She smiled. "You'll never believe this. Luna—the woman who owns the cat café—she offered me a job there."

"Wow, you're kidding!"

"I mean, I doubt I'll accept, but I'm flattered." She glanced at the café window. "We didn't discuss a salary or anything. It's probably silly for me to even consider her offer. I've got a business in Nocturne Falls and my sister." *A business that barely makes me enough to eat.*

"I hope you'll take this. It's perfect for you."

She laughed. "That's exactly what Luna said. Speaking of Nocturne Falls, I should really get back there today. I can't expect my twin to keep doing my job."

Sawyer stood up. "Let's go. We can be back before nightfall."

With a final glance at the café and a wave to the two cats in the window, she took Sawyer's hand and along with his cat, headed to her car for the trip back to Nocturne Falls.

She was going to miss Cat's Paw Cove.

Sawyer finished packing his toolbox after his first day back at the Tuckers' house. Glancing out the window at Jordan as she clipped lavender blooms and stuck them in a basket, he smiled. In a yellow dress and a big sunhat, she was lovely. He was falling in love.

His cell buzzed in his pocket. When he checked it and saw Sheriff Higgins's number on the display, he immediately answered. "Afternoon, Sheriff."

"How are you, Mr. Harrison?" the sheriff asked.

"I'd be better if you'd call me Sawyer." Although he was still getting used to the name, he liked it better than Harry.

"Deal. And you can call me RJ. I wanted to update you on the investigation."

Sawyer sat on the wingback chair. "Okay."

"Boris Komisky was transferred to the county jail. The DA interviewed him there. He admitted to being in Nocturne Falls last week. Unfortunately, he wouldn't own up to breaking into your house or truck there, or the one where Jordan was staying. But we've got him on several other charges, including assault and aggravated battery. Suffice it to say that Mr. Komisky will be a guest of the state for many years."

"Glad to hear it, Sheriff. What about my dear old aunt?"

"Thanks to Gladys, we're charging Angelica with attempted murder and embezzlement. She'll be locked away even longer than Komisky. If Parnell Jespers were still alive, he'd be locked up, too."

Relief coursed through him. He was finally free to go on with his life.

"Can I suggest something?" the sheriff asked.

"Sure."

"You've been through a lot. But you'll have control of all your assets back very soon. Take some time off to process and heal."

The idea of an extended vacation appealed to him. But if he couldn't talk Jordan into joining him, it wouldn't be very enjoyable. "Thanks for the advice, Sheriff."

"I hope we'll see you in Cat's Paw Cove soon. I ran into your cousin, Martine yesterday. She's hoping you'll move back here. And Luna over at Cove Cat Café said something about trying to lure Jordan here to work with the cats."

"I'll let you know. Thanks again."

Jordan came through the back door, her cheeks pink from the sun, and her feet bare.

She held up the lavender. "Aren't these beautiful? Smell."

He sniffed the flowers. "Absolutely gorgeous."Although he was referring to her, not the purple blooms. "I just spoke to Sheriff Higgins."

"What's up?" She set a tall glass vase in the sink and turned on the faucet to fill it.

He told her the news then sat at the kitchen table. "I've been thinking."

Jordan placed the vase in the middle of the table and joined him. "Okay."

"I'd like to move back to Cat's Paw Cove."

Her face was blank. He'd been hoping for her to be excited by his decision, and that she'd tell him she wanted to go, too. When she didn't say anything, he continued. "I'm going to relocate my business there. I have several relatives in the town, not just Martine. Apparently, the local veterinarian, Zane Anderson is another cousin, and there are others."

"That's...great."

He reached across the table and took her hand. "Would you ever consider moving there?"

A wry grin settled on her lips. "I was hoping you'd ask. Luna offered me a lot more than I'm earning here to manage the cat rescue. Honestly, it's my dream job."

He held his breath. This was too good to be true. But he didn't want her to have any regrets. "What about Mallory?"

Jordan pushed out of her seat and moved between his thighs, hooking her hands around his neck. "I'm hoping that after she and Cyrus tie the knot, they might think about relocating. She'd be a lot closer to Miami there. And since I happen to know that she wants kids, being four hours away from them would be a lot better than being a full day's drive, right? Who knows? I've got to live my own life regardless of what my sister decides."

"I must be dreaming." Sawyer reeled her in for a slow, sensual kiss. She tasted like fresh air and mint. He wasn't falling in love with her — he was already there.

EPILOGUE

Four months later…

Jordan fanned her fingernails to help the polish dry faster. Treating herself to weekly manicures felt so indulgent, but she'd been earning a decent amount of money for the past three months at the cat café. And in just a few days, Mallory would be moving to Cat's Paw Cove for her new job at Claws-N-Coifs salon.

"I can't wait until your twin sister gets here." Martine wiped down her nail table. "It's going to be awesome having a nail tech who also does tarot readings."

Martine had become more than just Jordan's manicurist — they were friends. Things had been going so well between Jordan and Sawyer, that someday, perhaps she and Martine would be related by marriage.

"Your haircut looks great, by the way," Martine commented. "Georgi is amazing."

Jordan nodded her agreement. Mallory had lamented that she'd miss the Hair Scare in Nocturne Falls, but Jordan had been right about her sister wanting to get pregnant soon. The newlyweds were already oohing an ahhing over every baby they saw. And Jordan was sure that Mallory would come to love this salon, and the rest of Cat's Paw Cove as well.

Martine glanced past Jordan and waved at someone. "She's ready for you, cuz."

Sawyer kissed the back of her neck. "And even more beautiful than she was a couple of hours ago."

Jordan's heart fluttered, as it did every single time Sawyer touched her. "Why, thank you."

"I'm taking this gorgeous creature out for lunch," he told Martine. "Want to join us?"

Martine rolled her eyes. "No thanks. Pardon me for saying, but you two are as nauseating as ten tons of lollipops."

Jordan chuckled. "I bet that Leo is looking for a date for the Valentine's Day Ball next week. Want me to tell him you're available?"

Martine held up her palms. "Heck no. Leo's a sweet guy, but I'm completely not interested in dating anyone, even him."

Jordan had noticed how Leo looked at Martine when she came into the café every morning for coffee, how he got all tongue-tied around her. Martine could deny that she liked Leo all she wanted. Jordan could spot a woman with a crush a mile away. "Whatever you say." She kissed Martine's cheek then waited as Sawyer gave his cousin a hug.

Taking Sawyer's hand, she waved goodbye to the rest of her new friends at the salon. "See you soon."

They walked to Purry's Burgers for lunch. The moment they went inside, Jordan inhaled the smell of the best burgers in town. Her stomach growled in response as they sat in their usual booth.

"So, speaking of the Valentine's Day Ball," Sawyer started.

Jordan set aside her menu. "Yes?"

"Mayor Watson asked me if you and I would join her at her table for the ball."

"Really? That sounds like quite an honor."

"I think it is."

Their waitress arrived with a tuxedo milkshake and two straws. "Do y'all want your usuals?"

Jordan nodded. "Thanks, Charlene."

After Charlene left, Sawyer eyed Jordan. "So what do you say? Should I tell Mayor Watson we accept her invitation?"

At first, when Sawyer had taken on a renovation project at the pretty redhead's home, Jordan had been the teensiest bit jealous. But after Sawyer had introduced her, and Jordan learned that the mayor was yet another of Sawyer's cousins, she'd relaxed.

"I'd love to," she told Sawyer.

"Good." He slid closer to her on the seat. "It's going to be a special night. And since your sister and brother-in-law will be here in a few days, I bought tickets to the ball for them."

"How exciting. I can't wait." Jordan could hardly sit still, and she suspected that was not only from the huge amount of sugar in the milkshake but also because Sawyer was planning something special for Valentine's Day.

He pressed a chocolate-flavored kiss to her lips. "It'll be a night to remember."

Her heart pounded. Sawyer had made her every dream come true, and the best part was that he said many times that she'd done the same for him.

Join Wynter Daniels and Catherine Kean in 2019 in

CAT'S PAW COVE

ABOUT THE AUTHOR

Wynter Daniels has authored more than three dozen romances, including contemporary, romantic suspense, and paranormal romance books for several publishers including Entangled Publishing and Carina Press, as well as for Kristen Painter's Nocturne Falls Universe. Along with author Catherine Kean, she will launch the Cat's Paw Cove series in 2019. She lives in sunny Florida with her family and a very spoiled cat named Chloe. After careers in marketing and the salon industry, Wynter's wicked prose begged to be set free. You can find her on the web on Facebook, Twitter and her website, www.WynterDaniels.com.

Also by Wynter Daniels

Beauty and the Bigfoot Hunter: Publisher: Sugar Skull Books, 6/2018

The Yin to His Yang: Publisher: Sugar Skull Books, 2/2018

The Genie's Double Trouble: Publisher: Sugar Skull Books, 9/2017

The Best Man's Proposal: Publisher: Entangled Publishing, 9/2017

The Fortuneteller's Folly: Publisher: Sugar Skull Books, 5/2017

Chasing the Stag: Publisher: W. Daniels, 11/2016

Emerald Intrigue: Publisher: W. Daniels, 11/2015

Shades of Sexy, Box Set: Publisher: W. Daniels, 01/2015

The Surrogate Husband: Publisher: Entangled Publishing, 12/2014

The Witches of Freedom Moon, Box Set: Publisher: W. Daniels, 04/2014

Dream Magic - The Witches of Freedom Moon, Book Three: Publisher: W. Daniels, 04/2014

Killer Magic - The Witches of Freedom Moon, Book Two: Publisher: W. Daniels, 10/2013

Hidden Magic - The Witches of Freedom Moon, Book One: Publisher: W. Daniels, 10/2013

Burning Touch & Tropic of Trouble: Publisher: W. Daniels, 4/2014

False Pretenses: Publisher: W. Daniels, 06/2011

Protective Custody: Publisher: Carina Press, 05/2011 (ebook & audio book)

Employee Relations: Publisher: W. Daniels, 04/2011 (ebook and print)

Game of Smoke and Mirrors: Publisher: W.
Daniels, 03/2011

8621

12382334R00119

Made in the USA
Middletown, DE
15 November 2018